BLAZE OF THE GREAT CLIFF

BLAZE OF THE GREAT CLIFF

Mark Fidler

iUniverse, Inc.

New York Lincoln Shanghai

Blaze of the Great Cliff

iUniverse, Inc.

For information address:
iUniverse, Inc.
2021 Pine Lake Road, Suite 100
Lincoln, NE 68512
www.iuniverse.com

ISBN: 0-595-28748-4 (pbk)
ISBN: 0-595-65847-4 (cloth)

Printed in the United States of America

Dedicated to my son Ross, who saw the great cliff dwelling,
and insisted that I write this story

CHAPTER 1

▼

Blaze wiped away the moisture from his forehead, and looked ahead. Ignoring the sting of salt in his eyes, he struggled to focus through his sweat blurred vision. The Great Cliff towered before him. He was back home.

"Great Spirit!" Blaze cursed. His legs ached, his feet throbbed and his lungs could not take in air fast enough. He had run as hard as he could, and for longer than ever before. And yet the Great Spirit had failed to send him a vision of his animal spirit. Blaze collapsed on the hard rocky terrain, and let his eyelids drop shut.

Only two hurdles separated Blaze from manhood in his Sinagua tribe. His animal spirit had yet to show itself to him, and he still needed his first large game kill. After that, he would be taught the sacred chants and rituals, and he would no longer be a child.

In one moon, Blaze would be off on his first journey. He was going to a land rich in large game, where he would surely make his big kill. After years of hunting rabbits and squirrels, Blaze dreamed of downing his first deer or antelope. A whole moon seemed like a long way off, but Blaze was patient and could wait.

Patience was one of the most important virtues of a great hunter. Blaze had learned patience from his countless gathering expeditions for Desert Cloud, the village healer, who always sought the precise plant, root or seed. While preparing for a hunt, many of the other boys in his village grabbed the first tree shoots they found, and used them before they had adequately dried. Those boys just wanted to start hunting sooner. They did not take sufficient time to ready themselves properly and so they never had great success. Couldn't they see that it was better to prepare slowly, even if it meant waiting longer to hunt? That way, when you finally did hunt, you nearly always came home with fresh game.

Blaze never rushed in his preparations. He not only crafted his arrowheads and shafts carefully, he even took great pains in choosing the feathers for his arrows. He preferred the black feathers of the crow. And Blaze was the only boy in his village who paid heed to which animal would provide the sinew for attaching his arrowheads and feathers to his bow shafts. He sought the muscle tissue of an animal great in spirit, an animal like the sleek, powerful mountain lion.

It was the spirit of the mountain lion that he had hoped would come to him on his run. Thoughts of his upcoming journey had momentarily erased the frustration of his empty vision. Thinking of the mountain lion, though, brought back his deep disappointment. The village elders had said that in order to see your animal spirit, you must run harder than you think possible, and at the point when your body can do no more, the vision of your animal spirit will come to you.

Blaze had run so hard that his legs and heart had nothing more to give. The harsh sun beat down on him, sapping him of the energy to get up and run another step. Why was Father Sun preventing him from going on? Why was Father Sun keeping his animal spirit away from him?

Blaze opened his eyes hoping that his animal spirit might have appeared. Instead, standing before him were the familiar gray ash and cottonwood trees of the plains, and beyond them, the Great Cliff. Built into the mountain of rock, his village home of nineteen rooms spread over five levels. The people on the cliff were mostly a blur to him. Even though he had stopped running, sweat continued to pour down his face and into his eyes. He wasn't sure if it was just sweat, or if tears of disappointment were mixed in.

It could be worse, Blaze said to himself. What if his animal spirit had appeared to him, and it was that of a rabbit? What kind of spirit would that be for a great hunter? But Blaze knew that people did not choose their animal spirit. A person is born with it and must discover that spirit within. Blaze prayed once again to Father Sun that his spirit was that of a hunter.

Next time Blaze would run even faster. He would spend more time in the sweatlodge, a tiny cave near the base of the Great Cliff. Many of the grand elders of the tribe used the sweatlodge to ease the aches and pains of old age, while Sinagua men and women of all ages used the room to purify themselves before life's important ceremonies. The older boys and younger men spent time there hoping to increase their running ability.

Mostly, plain hot water was poured over the stones, but sometime mesquite leaves or crushed beeweed was added. More than any boy in the village, Blaze understood the vast arrays of medicines from gathering the ingredients for Desert Cloud. He would be sure to speak to her and ask for a bath mix to enable him to run harder and faster.

Finally Blaze pushed himself up off the hard ground, and trudged along the rocky trail leading to the cliff. As he approached the lower ladder, the sounds of his people rained down on him like water from the clouds. The rhythmic, raspy chant of Golden Eagle echoed from the Great Room of the fifth floor. Golden Eagle was the oldest and most skilled weaver of the Great Cliff, and he always sang while making beautiful cloth for his people. The deep voice of his son Rattle Bone and the softer tone of Rattle Bone's son Hard Shell mingled in perfect harmony with the Golden Eagle's scratchy chant as the three men wove together. From lower in the cliff, White Snake's words rang with concern as she warned her young daughter to stay away from the edge of the walkway. At the same time, Blaze heard the playful cries of Tiger Eyes, Black Horn and Spadefoot as they chased one another around near the base of the cliff. The young children reminded Blaze of himself and his friend Setting Sun in the days when they were younger and had been allowed to play such games.

"Blaze going up to the lower ledge!" he called out as he stepped onto the stiff, woven rung of the ladder. He wearily pulled himself up to that ledge, and then on to the upper ledge in the same way.

"Blaze ascending to first floor!" he called after walking the ten paces along the upper ledge of the cliff.

"Come on up," Setting Sun called down.

Blaze pulled himself towards the first floor ledge. Beyond tired, his legs were almost numb. He let his arms do most of the work, practically pulling himself up each ladder rung. As he approached the ledge, Blaze heard the rattle of bone dice being shaken and falling on the smooth rocky floor.

"Want a game?" Setting Sun asked as Blaze's head appeared above the floor of the ledge.

Blaze shook his head as he pulled himself up onto the shelf of rock.

"I can lend you some beads," Setting Sun said. "Or I'll trade you thirty beads for one of your arrows."

"No way!" Blaze said. Give up an arrow for beads? That would be foolish!

"Okay, we can play for fun," Setting Sun almost whispered.

He must be pretty bored, Blaze thought. No one plays dice without something at stake. It was embarrassing. Blaze did notice that Setting Sun had lowered his voice intentionally when he had asked.

"No," Blaze said.

"I thought you were my closest friend, Blaze. Just one game."

"Setting Sun, you know that I don't like these dumb games. Why can't you just let me be? I thought that *you* were *my* best friend?"

Setting Sun let his eyes drop, looking both sad and ashamed.

"It's all right," Blaze said to his friend. "I do like to play dice sometimes. Just not now."

"Right. You like to play when you're on guard duty, and you have nothing else to do."

Blaze said nothing. That actually wasn't true. Blaze always brought plenty to do when he was on guard duty. He usually sharpened arrow heads.

"Where were you?" Setting Sun asked.

"I went running, remember?" Blaze answered, a little hurt that his friend could forget something so important. Then again, Setting Sun showed no interest at all in earning his own manhood. True, Setting Sun was one harvest younger than Blaze, but Blaze had been determined to achieve his Sinagua manhood for as long as he could remember.

"Oh, yes," Setting Sun said. "Did your spirit show itself?"

Blaze shook his head.

"Don't worry. Maybe your spirit will come to you on our journey. I think it will." Setting Sun spoke with a certainty that was almost eerie.

"How do you know?"

"I just have a feeling. That's all."

Blaze nodded.

"Much like the feeling that I had when I emptied your pouch of beads the last time we played dice," Setting Sun said in a teasing way, and laughed.

Blaze had tried to forget that game. It wasn't that the beads had meant that much to him. Many people in his village treasured their beads and shells, but not Blaze. It was that he hated to lose at anything. He believed that a great Sinagua had to constantly prove himself the best at everything he did, even at foolish dice games. And Blaze prided himself on doing nearly everything better than his friend Setting Sun, everything except gamble. Setting Sun always talked about these 'feelings' he got when he was betting. Maybe it was the God of the Wind whispering to him, as he claimed. And so, Blaze thought, maybe my spirit really *will* come to me on the journey, as Setting Sun believes.

Blaze tried to be hopeful, but he couldn't completely erase the disappointment that still lingered from the empty vision following his run.

"Setting Sun, I pushed myself more than I ever have! I ran so hard blackness almost came, but no spirit. I cannot run any harder."

"Trust my feelings, Blaze. And think about the hunt."

Yes, the hunt, Blaze thought excitedly. It would be his first major hunt, his first journey to the outside world. He smiled as he nodded to his friend, and called out his ascent to the second floor of the Great Cliff.

CHAPTER 2

▼

"Blaze, it is possible that your animal spirit was not ready," the hunched-over white haired man gently suggested.

"But Grandfather, maybe I could have run a little bit harder!"

"If what you tell me is true," Lion Heart said, "then you did run your hardest. You can do no more."

"Listen to your grandfather," Blaze's mother said as she seasoned the slate griddle with corn oil and roasted squash seeds. As the oil danced on the hot stone, she routinely said, "Great Spirit, bless this bread and the corn from which it is made."

As soon as Lightfoot finished her prayer, Bay Leaf spread a thin layer of piki bread batter on the hot griddle. Bay Leaf was Blaze's sister, and was one harvest older than Blaze. The smell of fresh bread jumped from the hot flat stone amid the spattering oil, overpowering the normally smoky smell of the cavelike room. Blaze loved fried bread, and for a moment, he forgot his disappointing run.

"Don't say anything to your father," Lightfoot said to Blaze.

"Why?"

"He already thinks that you're in too much of a hurry to become a man," Bay Leaf said bossily to her brother.

"That's not true," Lightfoot said to her daughter, and then turned to her son. "Blaze, it is only your wish to become a warrior which he discourages, and wisely so."

"But Grandfather tells so many stories about the glory of our great Sinagua warriors! Golden Eagle also talks of the same things."

"Blaze, those were in the early days, the days before all our people lived in the Great Cliff," Lightfoot said as she flipped the bread on the griddle, causing the dough to pop and sizzle. "The people of the earth are now at peace. And living in the Great Cliff, we are safe from invaders even if there is a war. Listen to me, Blaze. To survive these days, our people need to just grow food. Your father was blessed by the Spirit of the Corn, and he knows better than anyone in the village how to make it grow here. He simply wants to pass that knowledge on to you, his only living son."

As she said the word *living*, she bowed her head to the rear wall of the room.

"But I don't want to grow corn and squash and beans. I want to hunt, and I want to fight!" Blaze said.

"Great Spirit, forgive him," Lightfoot said quickly, and then her eyes moved to the ground. "Blaze, you must respect your elders. That is the first law of the Great Spirit."

"Grandfather is my elder, and Grandfather thinks that I will be a great warrior," Blaze stated.

"Is that correct, Elder Father?" Lightfoot asked Lion Heart.

"I simply suggest that we need to keep an open mind on the matter," the old man solemnly stated. "For many harvests now, our people have prospered thanks to the knowledge, skill and hard work of all of our people in the fields below. The Great Spirit has blessed us with good land and the knowledge to use it wisely. Perhaps that knowledge and skill will continue to keep our people safe and strong. Or perhaps less peaceful times will come, and the need for a warrior will be of greater importance. Also, should the fields become less plentiful, as they did at the well, then we shall rely more on the arrow than on the hoe."

"With all due respect, Elder Father, Great Bear has made clear that our young must first and foremost learn from the Spirit of the Land. And Great Bear is our Chief Elder. The Sinaguas of the Great Cliff must be farmers above all else."

"That is true, my daughter," Lion Heart said to Blaze's mother. "Still, we are people of the corn, yet we grow squash and beans as well. There are many gods, and we must be ready to please them all. We are people of the land, but must be prepared with the arrow to hunt game. And we must always be prepared to defend ourselves against invaders."

Lightfoot bowed to her father, and responded in a respectful tone. "The Chief Elder believes that only by showing complete faith in the Spirit of the Corn will our prosperity continue. The travelers have spoken of the poor harvests in the villages of the southern tribes. In recent times the Rain Spirits have not brought us many storm clouds, and even *with* rain, the soil sometimes seems to lose its spirit. Even our people at the well had to abandon their fields. Yet we are still more blessed than others. Great Bear has said that it is because we have stopped training our young in the art of the arrow that we have remained blessed."

"Like the seasons, spirits change," the old man spoke solemnly.

"Spirit of the Corn, forgive him," Lightfoot said with concern as she removed the bread from the griddle and spread two more sheets of batter on the hot stone surface.

Blaze was confused. He desperately wanted to continue learning the ways of the arrow. His grandfather had been secretly teaching him the skills of the warrior as well as those of the hunter. He had said that it was important that Great Bear and Dark Wolf and all the other elders not find out. But, Blaze thought, what if the Chief Elder is right? What if the Spirit of the Corn *is* offended? The past two seasons had brought less water down the creek than ever before. Maybe it was because Blaze and his grandfather had not put their complete trust in the Spirit of the Corn.

On the other hand, what if the Spirit of the Corn was losing power in the Great Underground? The spirits fight, as people do. And if the Spirit of the Corn and the spirits of the land lose in the struggles below, then Blaze's people will need to hunt more and maybe even fight in order to survive.

From outside, a deep voice rang out, "Swift Deer coming up to the fourth floor!"

There was silence in the room as each member of the family stiffened, afraid that Blaze's father might know the forbidden words that had just been spoken. They heard each step as Swift Deer moved up the ladder to the fourth floor ledge. The scraping of his yucca-fiber sandals against the ledge told all that he was up. They heard him march through the center room, where Coyote Claw and his family lived, and in moments, Swift Deer's head appeared through the tiny doorway. Blaze's father was a very large man, and it was with great effort that he squeezed himself through the tiny stone entrance. He sighed as he pushed himself into the room and stood there hunched, his shiny black hair grazing the ceiling of their low, dark room.

"The smell of corn on the griddle!" he boomed with a grin. "Nothing like it!"

Blaze's father said nearly the same thing each day as he returned from the fields. And it always brought a smile to his mother's face.

"Anasazi travelers have just arrived. From Bandelier, I believe," Swift Deer said.

"With baskets, I presume?" Lightfoot asked her husband.

"Of course. The villagers were saying that they were more beautifully decorated than ever."

Travelers! Blaze loved it when outsiders came to his village. They always brought news from the outside world as well as a wealth of interesting and uncommon items to trade. Anasazi were from the north and were known for their beautiful baskets and elaborately woven sandals. The Anasazi had many villages, with one that was bigger than ten Great Cliffs put together!

"How did you all pass the day?" Swift Deer asked.

"Blaze tried to see his animal spirit, but couldn't," Bay Leaf blurted to her father.

"Bay Leaf!" Blaze whined to his sister.

"Maybe if Blaze showed respect to the Spirits of the Land, then his animal spirit would show itself to him," Blaze's father said. There was a trace of anger in his voice. "He spends too much time away from the fields for a boy of fourteen harvests. He is not a child anymore, but if he acts like one, his animal spirit may never come to him."

Blaze felt a tug at his heart. What if his father was right?

CHAPTER 3

▼

"Blaze, don't lean out the window! Back away!" Lightfoot commanded.

"Mother, I am a Sinagua cliff dweller, and I am fourteen harvests old. Why do you speak to me as if I am a child?"

But Blaze knew the answer as he asked the question. The answer lay in the wall of their dwelling, the wall that held the bones and spirits of his two brothers. But it was only the eldest child who had fallen to his death. Blaze's older brother New Moon had just learned to walk when he teetered too close to the edge of the cliff and lost his balance. New Moon had died before Blaze was born. The second child, his mother's youngest, had died as an infant. Blaze was probably learning to walk himself when Dark Horse was born. Blaze couldn't even remember him. Dark Horse had lived for less than one moon before the Great Spirit had called him away from this world. All Blaze could remember was a great sadness in his home.

While Blaze had never known his brothers as people, he did know their spirits well. Because they had been children when they died, their spirits were not able to find their way to the Great Underground. With their bones buried in the wall of their cliff dwelling, the spirits of the boys would stay with the family until the day their mother died. At that time, she would lead them to the Great Spirit. Blaze felt the presence of his brothers in his home every day.

Blaze looked at his mother and saw the sadness in her eyes. He felt sorry for challenging her, and pulled back a little from the window. Peering down, though, he could still see the ground below. At the base of the cliff, two compact figures were visible. One Blaze easily recognized as the hunched over body of Setting Sun, probably rolling dice. The other figure wore a colorful band around his shiny black hair. It must be one of the travelers!

"I'm going down to see the visitors, Mother," Blaze said.

"Can you check on your little sister's dressing first?"

Blaze nodded. He stepped towards his mother as she turned away from him. Strapped tightly to the cradleboard on her back was Chittanberry, Blaze's infant sister of two harvests. Blaze unlashed the tie that held her upper body firmly in place.

Blaze knew that his mother kept her strapped in more tightly than necessary, but he also knew the reason why, so he did not dare say a word about it. Blaze had been tied in even more securely than Chittanberry, or so he had been told. No harm had been done to him, though. The back of Blaze's head was a little flatter than normal because it had been pushed so hard against his cradleboard, but Blaze liked the way his head was shaped. It was a mark of beauty among the people of the Great Cliff. Other cliff people were probably strapped tightly to boards, too, and have flat heads as well, Blaze thought. Either that, or lots of babies must fall from the cliffs to their deaths.

Blaze unwrapped the bandage covering his baby sister's burn, and gently pushed aside the wet dressing he had made from crushed yarrow plant. He could see that the burn was healing well.

"We can unwrap it in a day, and expose it to air," Blaze said to his mother.

Lightfoot nodded, and a moment later said, "By the way, Desert Cloud asked you to see her soon. She said that it was quite important."

Blaze responded with a slight nod of his head. Desert Cloud was the Great Cliff's medicine woman. She was even older than Lion Heart, Blaze's grandfather. The elders often said that Desert Cloud was born with the gift of healing. She was a wise and kind old woman, and seemed to know the name and healing powers of every plant and animal of the earth.

Blaze had spent much time with Desert Cloud, learning many skills in the art of healing. Desert Cloud had told Blaze that the mother of his Grandfather had been a great medicine woman. Without her skill and knowledge, the Sinagua men might not have survived their last war. That war had only been one battle, but many men had died, and most of the rest had been injured.

Blaze's father knew that Blaze did not share his love of the land, and so Swift Deer had always hoped that his son would be asked to train as a man of medicine. As Blaze had grown older, he had developed an interest in the art of healing, but the allure of hunting and fighting had remained stronger.

A medicine person spends much time traveling outside the cliff, seeking plants, roots, insects, and even animals for the slew of remedies needed by a tribe. When Desert Cloud was younger, she herself used to hunt small game for her medicines. She was now too old for that, and so she had the young boys hunt what she needed. Because Blaze had always been especially skilled with the bow, she had often asked for his help when she was in need of a squirrel or a rabbit.

"I'll make sure that I see Desert Cloud today, Mother," Blaze said as he stepped towards the door

Lightfoot nodded. "Do not be away long. We are eating soon."

Blaze walked through the door and into the large, open room of Coyote Claw and his family. Blaze nodded to Sharp Stone, a boy two harvests younger, and stepped past the three younger children playing on the floor. Everyone in Blaze's family had to walk through the room of their neighbor in order to get to the ladder and go down the cliff. It was important to respect the privacy of their neighboring family, and move through as quickly as possible.

"Descending to the third floor," Blaze called as he stepped outside and firmly grabbed the two side poles of the ladder to lower himself.

"Visitors!" Strong Horn called to Blaze from the large room in the center of the third floor. Strong Horn was Great Bear's son, and, like Blaze, was drawn to hunting and fighting. But Great Bear, the Chief Elder, was even more vocal than Swift Deer in his objections to any warlike behavior.

Blaze nodded to Strong Horn. He tried to avoid listening to the words spoken by the other families in their dwelling rooms, yet he could not help but feel the excitement that visitors always brought to the Great Cliff.

As he approached the base of the ladder, he heard Setting Sun's voice rise up the cliff.

"Are you sure you don't want to play one more time?"

"No, my parents will be angry when they hear how much I lost already. Any more, and I will be in even greater trouble."

The boy pronounced his words in a funny way, as travelers always did. He appeared to be close in age to Blaze and Setting Sun. Blaze couldn't take his eyes away from the boy's beautifully colored robe and headband. The yellows of the cloth jumped from the blues like a shining sun lighting up an autumn sky.

"Blaze," Setting Sun said, "this is Argus. He's a Chaco. He brought a basketful of beautiful beads to trade."

"Sounds like he has a lot fewer than when he started," Blaze said.

The young stranger turned his eyes away, trying to hide a look of shame.

"That's all right, Argus. He beats me all the time at dice too. Except it took me about three years of playing and losing before I figured out that I just shouldn't gamble with Setting Sun. It sounds like you figured that out a lot faster than I did."

The boy looked up and his big brown eyes softened as his mouth revealed the cracks of a smile.

"I'm Blaze. I'm a Sinagua, like Setting Sun. So, you're a Chaco?"

"Yes," the boy said. "We are part of the Anasazi people. Some people call us the Early People because the sun comes to us before any of the other Anasazi tribes."

"Do you travel a lot?" Blaze asked.

"No. This is my first journey."

"Setting Sun and I are going on ours in less than one moon. Where else are you going?"

"We are making a trip to the Great Water. They say that it is bigger than all the lands of the earth put together."

"We get lots of travelers coming from the Great Water," Blaze said. "And they always bring the most beautiful shells."

"Our jewelry makers are going to bring shells back to our village. We are also going to see if there is more water. There is not enough at home to grow our crops, and our village elders are looking for a new home, a home with more water."

"I thought that the Great Water was full of salt. Isn't it impossible for it to be used to grow corn and squash?" Blaze asked.

"We know that the Great Water cannot be used to nourish our crops," Argus answered, "but perhaps there is clear water, too."

"Is your village as big as I hear?" Blaze asked. "They say that the Chaco dwellings go on as far as the eye can see."

Argus laughed. "No, not nearly that big. But for every Sinagua in your Great Cliff, we have nearly one hundred Chacos."

One hundred! That was impossible!

"Yes," Argus said. "There are so many that I do not even know the name of each Chaco in my village."

Not knowing every person? That was hard to believe! Blaze knew the name of each person at the cliff. He even knew the name of every person who had died in his tribe, as far back as the elders remembered.

"But we have nothing as beautiful as the Great Cliff that you live in. You have five floors built higher into a cliff than I have ever seen. My friends back home will never believe it when I tell them of your Great Cliff. It's the most beautiful thing I have ever seen. You live up with the birds and the God of the Sun!"

Blaze turned around and looked up at his familiar home. The immense structure of buildings and ladders with so many ledges was amazing. Blaze didn't think about it very much, because it was the only home he had ever known. And he did often curse how long it took to go down to the creek and bring back water. Pulling the water baskets up the cliff walls was not one of Blaze's favorite chores. Still, the Great Cliff was safe, and warm in the winter, and the view of their land was spectacular.

"How about a game of rolling stones?" Setting Sun asked both Blaze and Argus.

"What, are you crazy?" Blaze asked.

Setting Sun shot Blaze a look of both anger and pleading.

"Didn't you hear our visitor say that he couldn't lose any more?" Blaze said. "You never lose at rolling stones!"

"Blaze!" Setting Sun protested.

"Argus, I'll trade you for some of those beads," Blaze said.

"What do you have?" Argus asked.

"I'll trade you an arrow head plus three pieces of argillite for ten of those blue beads."

"You're going to trade him one of your arrowheads? You never trade me one!"

"Setting Sun, stay out of it. I'm trading with Argus. You know that it is not polite to interrupt a negotiation between others."

"Can I see the arrowhead and rocks?" Argus asked.

Blaze reached into his pouch and pulled out a sharp, shiny black arrowhead.

"Wow!" Argus said.

"He makes the best arrowheads in the village," Setting Sun said proudly. "Blaze, why—"

"Setting Sun!" Blaze said sharply, afraid his friend would embarrass Argus. No one would want to be offered a favorable trade out of pity. That would be an insult.

Setting Sun drew his lips tightly together and shook his head in disgust at Blaze.

"It's a deal," Argus finally said, and they exchanged gifts.

"Guess which hand!" Setting Sun said to Argus as soon as he had the arrowhead in his hand.

"Huh?" Blaze asked.

Setting Sun held out his two closed hands.

"I have a piece of argillite in one hand and nothing in the other. Guess right, Argus, and I give you all your beads back. Guess wrong, and I get the arrowhead that you just traded for."

"Setting Sun, you can't—" Blaze started.

"My friend, it's not polite to interrupt the negotiations of others. Let me finish my business with Argus. What do you say, my young Chaco friend? All those beads back, and you will no longer be in trouble with your parents. I have only two hands. Chances are good that you win."

Blaze felt terrible for young Argus. The poor kid had already lost more than half of his beads, and had gotten nothing in return from Setting Sun. The only reason that Blaze had traded his arrowhead was that he had felt sorry for the young boy. But now he could say nothing.

He looked towards Argus, who wore an expression of pure anguish. Don't bet, Blaze thought. Maybe if I think hard enough, he will hear my thoughts.

"Okay," Argus finally blurted through pursed lips.

"No!" Blaze silently cursed. He hadn't meant for *Setting Sun* to have his arrowhead!

Setting Sun stared harshly at Blaze, who quickly turned away.

"Okay, which hand has the rock?" Setting Sun asked.

Argus stared and stared at Setting Sun's closed hands. He looked from one to the other. Setting Sun wiggled his left hand a tiny bit, as if he were adjusting a rock within. Blaze knew that trick well.

"That one," Argus said, pointing to the other hand, the one that had not moved.

Setting Sun kept both hands closed.

"Listen, if you're wrong, your parents might be quite upset. Give me two more beads, and we can call off the bet."

Blaze closed his eyes in disgust.

Argus shook his head no.

"Are you sure the rock is in that hand?" Setting Sun said.

Argus nodded yes.

"Open it!" Blaze ordered his friend.

Setting Sun opened his right fist. In his palm lay the chip of argillite. Argus had won! Setting Sun's other hand scooped up the pile of beads before him and he handed them to Argus.

CHAPTER 4

▼

"On your journey, I would like you to gather a number of plants from the Hohokam world," Desert Cloud instructed Blaze. "It has been many moons since we have traveled to that land, and there are a number of important medicines that need replenishing from plants abundant in that region."

Blaze nodded to the medicine woman.

"Wild onions are plentiful there, and are useful to us in insect season. They also have a variety of creosote bush that is especially effective in making the tea that I use to treat ailments of the stomach. I am low on beeweed as well, which looks like this."

In the sand the old woman scratched a picture of a weed with long, pointed leaves and a wide base. Blaze remembered what beeweed looked like from the last time travelers from Hohokam had come to the cliff, and Desert Cloud had traded for some of it.

"It is a light green, usually with brown tips at this time of the year. Bring as much of that as you can."

Blaze nodded. Desert Cloud went on to describe more of the many plants to be collected. He worked hard to memorize each one. Blaze knew how important these plants were to the making of the medicines, which were so essential to their tribe.

Blaze had always had an excellent memory and an uncanny ability to differentiate one plant from another. He assumed that was why Desert Cloud had so often asked for his assistance in collecting plants and roots.

"Before you return home, I ask you to seek Prongah, the Hohokam medicine man. Ask him to give to you any other plants that they have found useful since we last traded. He is a wise and good man and will be helpful. Do that just before returning, so that anything he gives will be as fresh as possible when you get back."

Blaze nodded again.

Desert Cloud returned to her work of sorting and mixing her newest medicines. Multitudes of small pots lined the thin ledges built into her wall. Painted on each pot was a symbol indicating a medicine or ingredient needed to make one of her salves, potions or teas. Desert Cloud could recite a long and complicated chant for treating each illness and wound. It had taken her many harvests to learn her art. Blaze knew the names and uses of most of the medicines, but did not know the accompanying chants. Only a medicine man or medicine woman in training could be taught those sacred chants, and the proper words were necessary for the medicines to be effective.

"And I did want to talk to you about something else," Desert Cloud said, as she carefully scraped off the outer layer from an agave stem.

Blaze listened but said nothing.

"It is time that I pass on my knowledge of the art of healing to a young apprentice."

Was she asking him to be that apprentice? There were few greater honors in the village. Only the Chief Elder was a more powerful and respected person among the people of the Great Cliff.

"You are blessed with many gifts, Blaze," the old women said as she pushed her long gray hair away from her eyes. Her dry, waist length hair covered most of her upper body and framed her face in an eerie shadow. "The art of healing is but one. I need to know if your heart would be in this noble calling."

She *was* asking him to be a medicine man! Blaze was deeply honored, but felt torn as well. He did feel a natural gift for healing and medicines, but the call to be a hunter and warrior was an even greater one.

"I understand your spirit, Blaze," Desert Cloud spoke. "Most young boys are drawn to the life of the arrow, but boys of the cliff grow to be Sinagua men, and the needs of the tribe must be considered. I am not asking you to decide right now. Go on your journey, and look into your soul. You have a good spirit. Trust it. It will lead you to the right path."

Blaze said nothing.

"Be off! I know that your grandfather awaits you."

How did she know he was going to see his grandfather? Did she know what they did together? If the village elders became aware of his secret training as a warrior, there would be great turmoil within his tribe.

Blaze stared deeply into the dark, sunken eyes of the ancient woman. Their spirits met, and then Blaze turned and left. Quickly, he made his way down one ladder after another to the bottom of the cliff, and then ran towards the east. He made his way past Red Canyon to a small open area surrounded by desert broom on one side and cliff snakeweed on the other. It was the place where Blaze usually met his grandfather.

The spry old man greeted Blaze with a raised right hand. Blaze bowed in return.

"I have two new short spears for you to take on your journey."

Blaze responded with a blank stare.

"You look distracted, my son."

"Yes, Grandfather."

"Sit down. Tell me about it."

Blaze seated himself on a nearby boulder. His grandfather sat down next to him.

"It's about Desert Cloud. She spoke to me about training as a medicine man." Blaze went on to tell his grandfather about the entire conversation.

"It is an honor to be asked to follow the path of medicine. There is no more important person in a tribe."

"But what about a warrior or a tribe's Chief Elder?"

The white haired man paused and said quietly, "Warriors are important in time of war. But anyone can be trained to fight. And a warrior has no power without a great person of medicine behind him. Even the Chief Elder must rely on a powerful medicine man or medicine woman. All decisions require the proper ceremony and the correct chants."

"Grandfather, I like medicine, but I love hunting and fighting."

"A man of medicine can be a hunter as well. When Desert Cloud was younger, she was one of the most skilled hunters in the village."

"But there are not any women who hunt now. Is it no longer allowed?"

"It is if she is a medicine woman. She needs to get just the right animals as well as plants for remedies. She knows better than anyone the spirit and healing power of the creatures she seeks."

Blaze struggled with these ideas. He knew how important a person of medicine was to his tribe. But he also knew that he wanted to be a hunter and a warrior. The legends of all tribes were filled with stories of the great warriors and battles, not with stories of medicine men. Blaze could see himself as a courageous warrior who leads his tribe to victory and is talked about for many harvests after he dies.

"Blaze, Desert Cloud is right. Do not concern yourself with this now. If you are meant to be a warrior, you will be a warrior. If you are meant to be a medicine man, you will be a medicine man. You need to be prepared with whatever skills your people will need. There are no young people trained in the art of war, and that is why I prepare you. Let the spirits steer you to your true destiny. For now, learn the art of the spear. Without it, you may never live to fulfill any other destiny."

Lion Heart held out one of the short spears.

"I thought that long spears were better hunting tools, Grandfather?"

"Hunting antelope and buffalo, yes. The long spear is best for large, slow prey. It is slower to release but pierces more deeply. The bow and arrow is valuable because it allows a man to keep his distance from the powerful beasts, but up close, or to drive a herd into a trap, the long spear works best."

"Then why do you give me these short spears?"

"Short spears are preferable in face-to-face battles with a quicker enemy, such as a leopard, or a mountain lion," the old man said, then hesitated, and quietly added, "or a man."

Blaze gulped. Would he be fighting soon? His grandfather had already taught him many important skills for war. He had taught him the most effective use of his head and knees and fists in hand-to-hand fighting. He had taught him how use a club or a rock to knock a man into blackness before he can utter a cry. Blaze's grandfather had also taught him the ways of the knife.

"Grandfather, I thought that the mighty cats like the leopard and mountain lion were scarce."

"They are, Blaze, but it always pays to be prepared. I am most concerned about other tribes."

"I thought that the people of the earth were all at peace?"

"They are, but this drought is a terrible one. The travelers say that the rains have dried up in other lands as well as Sinagua. Peace is easy in times of plenty, but amidst scarcity, we must be prepared for war."

Blaze nodded.

"Let us say that the saguaro over there is an enemy brave."

Blaze looked to his right. A giant green saguaro cactus stood facing him. Its wide central stalk with two upturned branches made it appear to be a giant, human enemy. It was almost frightening.

"The short spear is most effective when charging or when defending against an attacking enemy. To defend yourself, use an arrow to shoot the lead attacker. If the enemy is close, there is little time to properly mount another arrow onto your bow. That's when you use the short spear. After you have thrown your spears, reach for your long knife."

Blaze watched his grandfather demonstrate a throw of the short spear. Lion Heart moved with amazing smoothness and grace for such an old man. Approaching the cactus, he seemed to float through the air. He brought his right arm back and quickly stepped forward, and released the spear. The weapon struck the cactus exactly in the middle, where the branches went out from the trunk. It had landed right in the chest of the attacking warrior.

"You try," Lion Heart said.

Blaze grabbed the spear with his right hand, and lifted back his arm. He hefted the spear ever so slightly, acquainting himself with the feel and weight of the weapon. It had good balance. It would fly well.

As he approached the giant manlike cactus, Blaze could picture himself holding this weapon in the near future, ready to use it. His body tingled with excitement. More than ever, he was eager to go on his journey.

CHAPTER 5

▼

"Mother, I'll be back in one moon!"

"I know," Lightfoot said tenderly. "It's not that. You will return very soon, but a different you will come home."

The other adults in the great room nodded in knowing agreement. All the parents and grandparents of the three boys were present for the farewell ceremony.

"What do you mean? It'll still be me. Do you mean if I achieve manhood? I might not, you know."

"Oh, Blaze," Lightfoot said, holding her son's face in her small, dark hands. "I want you to become a man, and you will very soon. I know that you are a fine hunter and you will almost certainly kill your first big game, but whether your animal spirit chooses this journey to visit you or not, when you return, you will no longer be a child."

Blaze desperately wanted to be a man of his tribe, but the way his mother spoke made him sad. Sad for her and sad for himself. Would he someday wish to be a child again? Setting Sun's father Tall Grass was always saying, 'Oh, to be a boy again,' whenever he saw his son playing any sort of game. Blaze certainly hoped that he would not feel that way some day. Not after a lifetime of praying to become a man.

"Don't make the boy feel bad about growing up," Swift Deer said to his wife. "The sooner he is a man and forgets about playing the games of children, the better for him and for the whole tribe."

"Swift Deer, this is our baby boy. It seems like only yesterday that he was strapped in the cradleboard, gurgling and smiling and reaching for anything near to him."

"He was a different person then," Swift Deer snapped too loudly and with too much anger, "and he had better be a different person when he does return from this journey. I don't even remember him in that foolish cradleboard! Men do not notice babies."

Blaze was suddenly overwhelmed with feelings of hurt and confusion. Why was his father so angry? Was it only because his son did not like to work the fields?

"Swift Deer," Lightfoot said, "you don't remember because you would not look at him until he was many harvests old. But you were never able to take your eyes away from New Moon when he was a baby. When he died, no one was more devastated than you were. I think that you are still grieving and have not noticed that you have a beautiful son who is healthy and alive. He is about to start a life of his own, and you have missed his time with us!"

A hush spread over the large room. Drowning in strange, new emotions, Blaze was speechless. He had never heard any of that about New Moon, and did not know what to think. He glimpsed about and saw Setting Sun's father and brother turning nervously aside. Spear Thrower's family was awkwardly gazing away as well. Blaze glanced at his older sister and saw Bay Leaf cupping her hands in front of her eyes. He looked more closely at her and noticed a tear running down her left cheek.

"Come, now," Lion Heart said with calmness and authority. "This is a family celebration. Three boys are about to go off on their first journey. There is always sadness, but it is a time for joy, especially for these boys. We adults must not let our emotions get the better of us. I do believe Deer Eyes has made a special treat for us."

Ever since Blaze had entered the Great Room, Spear Thrower's mother had been busy doing something by the rear wall. Would she provide yet another great remembrance from his favorite room in the cliff? The large fifth floor room held so many special memories for Blaze. Even though it was the biggest room in the Great Cliff, nobody lived there. It was too large to heat adequately, but it also was the only room big enough to hold everyone in their village. The Dance of Rain took place there each harvest. So high on the cliff, they were as close as possible to the clouds and to the Rain Spirits. Mating ceremonies as well as coming of age ceremonies took place in the Great Room, too. With only three families sharing this special celebration, the big room seemed more spacious than ever.

"Is your mother making food?" Blaze quietly asked Spear Thrower.

Spear Thrower shrugged his shoulders indicating that he did not know.

"I sure hope it's food," Setting Sun said.

"You mean, you have not eaten enough?" Spear Thrower asked.

They had just finished an enormous bean and meat stew. Mixed in with deer was the meat of a fox that Dark Wolf had recently shot. The stew, along with both corn bread and squash bread, had been delicious and very filling. But Blaze felt that a celebration was not complete without a special sweet something on the tongue before the end. He wondered what it would be.

"Be satisfied with what you had," Spear Thrower added.

It bothered Blaze that Spear Thrower was always acting so much like an adult. Even though Spear Thrower was just thirteen harvests of age, like Setting Sun, he took farming and his household responsibilities as seriously as Swift Deer did! That's why Blaze and Setting Sun spent little time with him, even though he was one of the few boys near to their age in the village.

"Mother is ready," Strong Ribs announced in a bossy voice. Strong Ribs was Spear Thrower's sister, and acted as if she were a woman of thirty harvests rather than a girl of fourteen.

"Ay-yah!" Spear Thrower's little brother Spadefoot cried.

Everyone's attention was drawn to Deer Eyes, who was slowly pulling a blue woven tapestry away from the rear wall of the oversized room. Blaze wondered why she would store food up on that wall.

And then he saw it. It was so beautiful it nearly took his breath away. Deer Eyes had not been preparing food. There on the large stone wall, staring back at the three boys and their families, were Blaze, Setting Sun and Spear Thrower. Not the real boys, but a painting, actually. It was a spectacular, life-size wall painting. The giant image of the three boys seemed to jump from the wall. Their hauntingly realistic eyes held the stare of every person in that room. No one said a word for a long time. Finally, Blaze spoke.

"Thank you," he said quietly. Deer Eyes regularly recorded major events of the Great Cliff through wall paintings, but never one like this.

"It is magnificent," Setting Sun said.

"Most wonderful," Spear Thrower added.

"I have nothing as wonderful for you, my dear son" Lightfoot said to Blaze, "but I did make a sweetbread with raisins from the Chacos for you to take on your journey. Please share it with Spear Thrower and Setting Sun."

Sweetbread! With raisins! Even though his stomach was full, the thought of sweetbread with raisins caused Blaze to salivate.

His journey was so close, he could hardly believe it. And of all the destinations, the Hohokam world was the best. Besides being known for their beautifully painted pottery, the Hohokam were famous for their ferocious games of ball. They had built countless arenas for their games, each arena bigger than every room in Blaze's village put together. And the Hohokam people used to be a tribe of great warriors, before the days of peace had come.

"And I have something for you as well," Swift Deer said, interrupting Blaze's thoughts. The giant man reached into his breech sack and pulled out a shiny yellow object. He handed it to Blaze.

Attached to a string was a bright piece of metal carved into the shape of a shining sun. It was a necklace!

"This amulet was made by the people of the Great Water. It is sculpted from a metal they call gold. They say Father Sun is made of hot gold, the holiest of all metals. Wear it always, my son."

Blaze nodded. He was moved almost to tears.

"I will," he tried to say, but the words would not come.

CHAPTER 6

▼

"That way!" Setting Sun whispered loudly to Blaze, pointing to the thick brush to their left.

Heart pounding, Blaze led his friend slowly towards the origin of the noise. He was happy to be off with only Setting Sun. Spear Thrower had joined three of the men in search of big horn sheep. While those large sheep were not ferocious, they were skilled cliff climbers. Because they could ascend a cliff so quickly, and even jump down four man-lengths onto rock, they were very difficult to hunt. No other animal of such size would dare leap that kind of distance, but it is said that big horn sheep used to have wings, and still believe they have them. The other men on the journey had headed for the wooded region to the west in search of deer. But Blaze had wanted to hunt buffalo and antelope, animals that could fight back, and so he and Setting Sun had gone to the plains seeking their prey.

They approached the thick, round cluster of desert broom and slowly stepped around it.

"It's gone," Blaze said as his eyes searched the rocky landscape. "Are you sure it was a deer?"

"I know what a deer looks like, and I know it was a deer."

"That's what some Mogollon hunter said."

"What do you mean?" Setting Sun asked.

"Don't you remember when the Hovenweep visitors came last year? They were telling us about how they hunted deer. Their fastest hunters disguised themselves as deer to get close to the real ones, and then they could steer the deer in the direction of the other hunters. Anyway, one of the hunters wore a disguise that was so realistic that he was shot by one of his fellow tribesmen!"

Setting Sun grinned.

"What's so funny?" Blaze asked. "The hunter was killed!"

"If it's not funny, why are you working so hard to hide your grin? It's showing at the corners of your mouth."

Blaze let himself smile, and said, "You're right. Even though it's sad, it is funny, too."

Blaze relaxed the hand holding his bow and let his weapon fall to his side. "I guess that I won't be getting my big kill today after all. And this is the sixth day of our journey!"

Blaze hoped that Spear Thrower had been no more successful. It was wrong to wish that, Blaze knew, especially with the need for fresh meat so great. Still, Blaze wanted to be the first of the three boys to make that first big kill.

"Don't sound so sad," Setting Sun said to his friend. "It's only the second day we have hunted. I haven't shot anything either."

"Sh!" Blaze hushed, pointing ahead to a cluster of low lying brush behind a giant saguaro cactus.

The two boys ducked behind a rock. Blaze drew back his arrow, pulling the sinew as far back as he could. Setting Sun quietly slipped an arrow onto his bow as well. They both heard a loud rustling sound come from the dry saltbush. There was definitely a large animal in there!

This could be it, Blaze thought, searching the faded green foliage of the shrub for the darker fur of his prey.

To his left, Blaze spotted a slight movement of a willow leaf branch. He aimed his arrow at that spot. Setting Sun did the same, ready to fire.

"Not yet!" Blaze whispered. "We need to see the animal first. Otherwise, we'll only frighten it and drive it away."

Setting Sun nodded.

Patience, Blaze thought. A great hunter must have patience, and Setting Sun does not have patience, but I do.

Holding his arrow, prepared to shoot, the thrill of the hunt's final moment welled up inside him. The shot itself, though, was only a small part of the whole adventure. Blaze loved every part of the hunt. Searching for the right stone to carve into an arrowhead was the first step, and one that he took very seriously. He would spend hours scouring the creek and the base of the cliff for the perfect stone, and then carefully shape it until it was sharp and properly balanced. Finding good tree shoots for his arrow shafts was also important. Choosing the best ones made him feel grown up. Blaze knew that hunting was more than simply aiming and firing an arrow. Just as important was crafting the perfect tools to assure success in his hunts. Blaze always chose more shoots than he needed. That way, after peeling them and bundling them to let them dry, he could pick the straightest ones for his arrows. Pride tingled from his fingertips as he ran them down his well crafted arrow.

Suddenly, a high squeal sounded from behind the willow leaf bush. And it was not the sound of a deer!

A high shriek rang out next, followed by the word, "Here!"

At that instant, a child ran out into the open. He must have been the one who scared the deer away! The young boy held a round object unlike anything Blaze had ever seen. It was soft and brown, and about the size of a human head. Was it a shrunken head? Blaze shuddered. He had heard tales of tribes that saved and shrunk the heads of their dead.

Blaze and Setting Sun each lowered their bows as they ducked behind the large rock before them. This must be a Hohokam boy, Blaze thought. His group had expected to see the first of the Hohokam the next day when they approached the Gila River. The word

Hohokam meant 'bean eater.' They were called that because they planted so many mesquite beans. As Blaze peeked at the young person through a crack of the boulder in front of him, he wondered how many beans this boy had eaten.

A louder noise sounded from behind the boy. A bigger person seemed to be working his way through the shrub, towards the child. Except it was not a *he*. It was a *she*! A long legged girl with shiny black hair appeared and approached the young boy. Her fine hair hung freely to her lower back and her smooth skin was the color of ripe winterberry. As she smiled at the boy, Blaze gasped. He had never seen such a beautiful girl.

Her eyes darted towards Blaze and Setting Sun. Neither boy moved a muscle. The girl grabbed the young child's hand and cautiously stepped towards the rock that hid Blaze and Setting Sun. She must have heard us, Blaze thought. And it was me that she heard! He was disgusted with himself. Blaze prided himself on total self control in the face of danger, but a young girl's beauty had caused him to give away his position! No wonder his animal spirit had not yet come to him. What kind of hunter was he?

Setting Sun lay flat behind the rock while Blaze kept one eye exposed, peeking through a crack between the two boulders forming the large rock before him. He was afraid if he moved, then she would see and hear him. Also, he did not want to stop looking at her. And then he felt her eyes meet his. She stopped as her eyes opened wide with concern. Her hand instantly squeezed the hand of the child even more firmly. Without taking her eyes from Blaze's, the girl began to step backwards. The child must have sensed her concern, because the muscles of his face tightened into a nervous grimace.

Should I say something? Blaze thought. Or should I let her walk off?

"Wait!" he finally called out, stepping into the open. He held both arms out to his side in the standard gesture of friendliness.

The girl's eyes went straight to the bow and arrow that he was still holding, and she turned around and ran.

"We're in trouble now," Blaze said.

"What do you mean?"

"What would you do back home if you were out and saw two boys armed with bows?"

"Oh, no. You're right!" Setting Sun said. "They'll be searching for us soon."

"So let's follow them, but go up around to the right over there. They'll come straight back to this spot, and then assume that we ran off in the opposite direction, and so they'll probably look for us back there."

"I thought that the Hohokam were a friendly people?" Setting Sun asked. "These must be Hohokam, right?"

"Yes," Blaze said, "they must. And they are supposed to be friendly, but I would rather let the elders in our group make first contact. That girl looked quite scared when she saw our bows. Who can guess what she will tell her elders."

"You're right. Let's go."

The two boys ran in the direction that the girl had headed, veering slightly to the right, as they had planned. Blaze moved quickly and quietly while Setting Sun dragged his feet on the ground, creating a constant shuffling noise. Blaze had learned from his grandfather how to move rapidly and with almost no sound. It was an important skill for a warrior.

After running for a while, Blaze held a hand up towards Setting Sun. They both stopped. Voices from a crowd of people echoed in the distance. Blaze had never heard so much yelling and shouting. It sounded like children playing, but the voices seemed too deep to be those of children. Blaze cautiously advanced towards the commotion. On the other side of some snakeweed and elderberry shrubs was a huge clearing. Blaze and Setting Sun ran up to the shrubs and spread apart the dry branches to see through to the other side.

It was a fight! One man was running, holding onto one of those round, brown things that the boy had been holding. Enemy warriors were chasing him while others were protecting the man. Suddenly a small, quick warrior broke through the protection, and slammed into the man with the brown thing, popping it loose.

As it rolled forward, four men dove for it. Blaze noticed a group of older men along with women and children standing at the edge of the battlefield, calling out encouragement and praise.

And then it hit Blaze. They weren't fighting. It was a game, like young Sinagua children play! And the object must be a ball! He had heard about the great Hohokam ball arenas. This must be one of them!

Blaze scanned the playing area and realized that the contest was taking place on a huge, egg-shaped arena sunk into the ground. The people watching were all standing outside the dug out area while the competitors were positioned inside.

Blaze guessed that the youngest ones were a little older than he was while the oldest seemed a little older than his father. There were no grand elders out there. Each competitor's bare upper body was heavily adorned by paint, and protected by leather padding tied about the shoulders. Below the waist, only a breechcloth was worn, with more padding wrapped around the shins. On their feet, the men wore heavy sandals tied securely around their ankles. Blaze realized that half of the men were painted red and half were blue. The color must determine who was in which tribe.

A tall blue painted man was running with the ball. His forearms held it tightly against his chest with his hands clenched into fists. As a red enemy streaked in from the left, the man in blue popped the ball into the air and punched it forward with his fists. Immediately after, he was slammed to the ground, but he had safely released it before being hit.

The brown ball sailed high and landed perfectly into the arms of a short blue boy running at an incredibly fast speed. He caught the ball without slowing down a step. It was beautiful! The throw had led him perfectly, like an arrow shot ahead of a running animal.

All alone, the short man in blue ran to the end of the arena and tossed the ball up into a large woven basket built into a sturdy frame of wood. After the ball fell through, his tribemates surrounded him, patting him on the back and singing praise. The women, children and elders on the side of the arena cheered as well.

Blaze's heart pounded with excitement. The game was like a war, but not like a war. It was incredible! Blaze had never seen anything like it. No adult in his village had ever competed in any games, yet Blaze knew that this was something that he had to do.

"Don't move!" a voice barked from behind.

Blaze and Setting Sun turned their heads and found themselves facing the drawn arrows of four strange and unfriendly-looking boys.

CHAPTER 7

▼

"They're just flatheads," one of boys said. His words sounded a little different from the way people spoke in the Great Cliff, but Blaze understood him, as he usually understood visitors to his home.

"Put down your weapons," another boy commanded. He pronounced his words in the same harsh way.

Blaze and Setting Sun slowly placed their bows and arrows on the ground. The Hohokam boys continued to aim their arrows at their captives.

The boy who had first spoken picked up one of Blaze's arrows. "Well made," he said. "Maybe there is some intelligence inside one of those flat heads after all."

Flat heads. The boy spit out the words, making a flat head sound like a terrible thing. With Blaze's people, having a flat head was considered a sign of beauty. Most people born in the Great Cliff had flat heads because when they were babies, their mothers had carried them on their backs, strapped tightly onto a stiff cradleboard. So high on a cliff, it was essential that a child be held securely, otherwise disaster could result. A good mother was particularly careful, and tied her baby in especially tightly. As a result, the soft skulls of newborn babies tended to flatten out from being pushed so hard against the rigid board.

"Flatheads, do you have names?" a third boy asked.

Blaze stared defiantly at the four boys. Setting Sun looked towards Blaze to see how to respond, and then remained silent himself.

"Yes, this is quite well made," said the boy who had picked up the arrowhead as he examined it. "This will provide a good memory of our first encounter with flatheads."

"No, Bravegart," another boy said. "Our elders would be unhappy. Our village was expecting Sinagua travelers on a trading journey. These boys must be from that tribe."

"Lontooth, only *some* of our elders would be displeased. Others would be quite content to have us improve our supply of arrows."

"Bravegart," another boy said, "Lontooth is right. It is not our place to cause trouble for our village. If we want arrows, we must trade for them. Otherwise, we must return them to these Sinagua boys."

"Phpht!" Bravegart spit out. "Okay, Stonah, a trade it is. You give them one of your feathers. A feather for an arrow. That seems to be a fair trade to me. And if our guests do not object, then I take it that they agree to my terms."

Stonah, who seemed like a nicer boy, hesitated as he reached for a feather attached to his waist strap.

"Give them the feather!" Bravegart commanded.

Stonah slowly pulled out a long white and blue one.

"Give it to the flathead!"

"No!" Blaze said firmly. "I will not trade one of my arrows for just a feather!"

Setting Sun looked nervously towards his friend, and then turned back towards the armed Hohokam boys.

"A courageous one, I see," Bravegart said. "Maybe I was wrong about brains in those flat heads. If I were outnumbered in a strange village by four boys armed with arrows, I would agree to any reasonable terms."

"But those terms are not reasonable, and you know it," Blaze said.

The three boys eyed Bravegart, looking for a clue as to how to react. The tall Hohokam finally shook his head and said, "Their loss. Everyone knows that Snaketown feathers are the most valuable in the world. Let them walk away from a good deal."

Blazes's arrow was tossed onto the ground as Bravegart turned around and marched off. Two of the boys followed. Only the smallest one, the one they called Stonah, remained.

"I apologize for my people," Stonah said quietly. "Bravegart is not always so unfriendly."

Blaze nodded.

"My name is Stonah. What's your name?" he asked. "Are you from Sinagua?"

"Yes, we are," Blaze answered. "We are the Sinagua people of the Great Cliff. I am Blaze, and this is my friend Setting Sun."

"The Great Cliff!" Stonah exclaimed. "I have heard tales of the Great Cliff of Sinagua! They say that it is built into a cliff as high as the sky. Is that true?"

"Our Great Cliff is beautiful," Setting Sun said. "It *is* high in the sky, close to Father Sun."

"I have always wanted to see it," Stonah said. "I hope to go on an expedition to see your Great Cliff someday."

Blaze's eyes were drawn back to the ongoing ball competition in the distance.

"Do your people play guayball?" the young Hohokam boy asked.

"Huh?" Blaze said.

"Guayball. The game they're playing."

"It's called guayball? No, our people play no games. Young children kick balls and chase one another, but older children and adults do not play games. The field work takes most of our time. And our elders say that games encourage warlike behavior. We are a peaceful people."

"You have no guayball arenas at all? Every one of our villages has its own ball arena, and the bigger ones have two! All of our men play guayball."

"Our elders think that adult games are foolishness," Blaze said. "They are an insult to Father Sun, who expects us to use his gifts to grow food."

Stonah laughed. "I think that I like our gods better than yours!" he said. "Guayball is our way of worshiping the gods! By imitating the contests between them, we show our respect. The young men play while the old men make wagers on the games."

"Wagers!" Setting Sun repeated excitedly.

"Oh, yes! A village with a good guayball pod lives quite well!"

"Pod?" Blaze asked.

"Pods. Groups of people who play together."

"Oh, I see," Blaze said. "Like bean pods."

"Yes. Like the peas inside the pod, they are one. And for the past two years, Snaketown's East pod has been the best of all the Hohokam villages. We did not lose a game. It has kept our bellies full with an abundance of food. And extra furs have kept us warm in the winter. Beautiful beads and feathers decorate our homes as well, all from our success with guayball. Look! There is Greatgart with the ball. He is Bravegart's father, and he is the fastest and strongest player in our village's West pod. I think that he is the best in the whole Hohokam world. We were fortunate our East pod was able to stop him."

Blaze had not taken his eyes away from the action, even as he listened to Stonah's every word about this incredible game. Blaze had already realized that Greatgart was the best player. Greatgart was tall, strong and handsome, except for his round head, and when he ran, his long legs looked like the perfectly muscled hind legs of a magnificent galloping horse.

Greatgart was sprinting up the right side of the arena as four red painted players angled over to intercept him. There was no way that he could beat them, and he was too far ahead of any of the other men on his pod to get their help. Suddenly Greatgart faked right and cut left, sending two of his pursuers to his right and out of the playing arena. Greatgart then punched the ball straight up into the air. The two men following him had not expected that move, and could not help but run past the ball as it came down, their arms flailing desperately for it. Greatgart instantly stopped, letting his pursuers fly by him, and caught the ball himself as he cut towards the center of the playing area.

The four other men in blue were cutting in to meet him in the middle of the arena when Greatgart popped the ball up with his forearms, and his two fists punched it perfectly to a red podmate far to the left. Just as each of the blue painted opponents approached that man, Greatgart's podmate sent the ball back to the center of the playing area where Greatgart was sprinting to meet it. He caught it perfectly in the crook of his bent arms and ran freely to the end line. He stopped and tossed the ball ahead, raising his fists in celebration as it dropped through the basket.

"They say that Bravegart is going to be an even better player than his father," Stonah said.

"When will he be able to play?" Blaze asked.

"Next year, when he comes of age."

"Do young people ever play this guayball?"

"Of course! But only amongst children of the same village."

"And do young people wager on those games?" Setting Sun asked eagerly.

Blaze laughed to himself. Of course Setting Sun would ask that question.

"Something must always ride on a competition," Stonah replied, as if it was the most obvious answer in the world.

Setting Sun smiled.

Blaze worked up the courage to ask the next question. He did not know if it was an appropriate thing to bring up, but he needed to ask anyway.

"Are visitors from another tribe ever allowed to participate in your games for young people?"

"We are required to include visitors we invite into our homes."

Blaze's eyes lit up. Stonah was studying the face of his new friend, and seemed to read his mind.

"Would you like to share bread with my family tonight?"

An invitation to eat meant that he was also invited to play this game of guayball! Blaze wanted badly to say yes. He looked to Setting Sun.

"I don't know, Blaze. We've been gone for a long time now. The sun is getting low. Our people might be concerned."

"But Setting Sun, hunters are always expected to follow up their chase. Hunters often return after dark and no one ever worries."

"Adult hunters," Setting Sun said.

"I guess you are right. We should decline this invitation. Maybe we will be invited again when we visit this tribe in future harvests. I can try this guayball then, and you can wager on the contest."

Setting Sun paused.

"No," Setting Sun said, nodding his head towards Stonah. "Blaze, I think maybe you were right in the first place. No one will be concerned. Plus, we would not want to insult this kind host of ours."

Stonah nodded back and smiled.

"Then let's go!" Blaze cried.

CHAPTER 8

▼

Walking with Setting Sun under a hazy morning sun, Blaze could not wait to see Snaketown. He had heard much about the enormous Hohokam village and was eager to see it. They followed the route Stonah had described and in no time, they were there.

Blaze stared wide-eyed at the open marketplace. Throngs of people crowded the artisans who were selling and crafting their wares. There were more people at the market than were in Blaze's entire tribe! Young children screamed as they ran and played, while the adults exchanged news, laughed, argued and sang. Studying the market before him, Blaze counted fifteen low stony mounds surrounding an open area floored with large manmade squares of rock. Between mounds, Hohokam men and women were preparing food, shaping pottery, chipping stone weapons and tools, and creating jewelry. On top of the mounds, crowds of young people surrounded the weavers.

"It is good to see you, my friends," Stonah said, appearing behind Blaze and Setting Sun.

"It is good to see you," Blaze said.

"What do you think of Snaketown?" Stonah asked.

"It is quite spectacular," Blaze said.

Setting Sun nodded in agreement, and then asked, "The *women* weave in your village?" Setting Sun's father was one of the most respected weavers at the Great Cliff.

"Yes," said Stonah.

"In our village, it is only the men that weave," Setting Sun said.

"It used to be only men here, but more and more of our men were needed to travel forth on hunts and to extend our canals since the God of the Rain has become less generous."

"Why do they work on top of those mounds?" Blaze asked.

"Only weavers may practice their craft on the plaza's elevations," Stonah said. "Those who weave are our most holy people. Long before any other village had learned the art of weaving, the Hohokam were chosen to be the people of the cloth. All other tribes traded their best goods to get Hohokam woven material. We had good land for cotton, and our people learned to spin and dye beautifully colored threads. From those, they weave the most beautiful garments in the world. Look at all the children surrounding the men and women at work. There is no higher calling for a Hohokam child than to be asked to apprentice as a weaver. Every three harvests, a weaver will choose a new apprentice to learn the art of the cloth. A child is chosen who has shown great interest and skill."

Blaze noticed the intensity of the children who were watching the elder weavers. They were clearly competing to be chosen as the next apprentice.

"They would rather weave than play guayball?" Blaze asked.

"Actually, many would rather play ball, and it disturbs some of the elders. They fear that it represents a return to our days as warriors instead of craftsmen. Many of our own people fear Greatgart."

"Greatgart is a strange name," Blaze said. "What does it mean?"

"Gart is our greatest god, god of the garth, which is soil."

"What does Stonah mean?" Setting Sun asked.

"Stonah is the god of stone. In this city of rock, Stonah is a most special name. But all Hohokam names are borrowed from our gods.

We return those names to our gods when our time in this world is done. Some believe that those who die in battle bring great glory to the god of their name."

Blaze shuddered at the thought of fighting against the Hohokam, and especially against Greatgart. Even his son Bravegart would be an intimidating foe. Blaze was glad that the Sinaguas and Hohokam were friendly trading partners.

"Stonah," Setting Sun said. "Stop! Let me see this."

Setting Sun squeezed his way through a crowd of adults and children surrounding a very old man. Blaze followed. The man had long white hair hanging down his upper back like a pony's tail. His bluish-gray eyes were buried in the deep wrinkles of his dark, leathery face. His spotted dark hands looked older than the earth itself, and yet he moved those fragile hands with the skill of a master weaver from the Great Cliff. Blaze saw that the ancient artist was carving a beautiful design of overlapping circles on a large shell. To the man's side lay other smaller shells adorned with inlaid chips of shiny, bright stones. Blaze knew that the shells must have come from the land of the Great Water.

"Wow, beautiful!" Setting Sun said.

Stonah moved between Blaze and Setting Sun.

"What's in that pot there?" Setting Sun asked Stonah.

"Pitch."

"What about that?" Setting Sun asked, pointing to a clear liquid in a red and brown pot on the ground.

"That's fermented cactus juice. Long Horn soaks the whole thing in that at the end. The young men sometimes get in trouble for stealing that fermented juice and drinking it. It makes them wild."

Blaze smiled. Setting Sun paid no attention to the non-artistic uses of the cactus juice. Instead, he studied each movement of the old man at his work. Blaze noted Setting Sun's trance-like awe over the decorated shells. Most of the time, Setting Sun wagered jewelry in his games. He had amassed quite a collection and had developed a real appreciation for decorative beads and shells.

Blaze spotted a younger man carving arrowheads at another station. Leaving the old man and the shells, he approached the other craftsman chipping away at his piece of brown stone. The arrowhead maker was about ten harvests older than Blaze, and was working with great concentration. Four finished arrowheads lay on the mat next to the man as he labored. His eyes did not veer from his work, even as Blaze leaned over to examine the arrowheads.

"You may pick them up and look," the man said without glancing up.

Blaze took one and held it in his open palm, rocking his hand slightly. The arrowhead was longer and thinner than the ones Blaze usually made, but it was well balanced.

"It doesn't look as good as yours," Setting Sun whispered to Blaze.

Blaze turned around and shot an angry glance at his friend. What if the man had heard Setting Sun? One should never insult a serious artist, especially one from another tribe.

"I have never seen one shaped like this," Blaze said to the dark haired man.

"We use them to hunt antelope," the man said, finally looking Blaze in the eye. He spoke quietly but there was a seriousness and intensity in the man's eyes, which startled Blaze. It was very different from the gentle wisdom that Blaze had seen in the eyes of the old man decorating shells.

"Do you hunt?" the man asked.

"Yes, but mostly small game, like rabbits and rock squirrels. This is my first hunt for big game. Setting Sun and I almost killed a deer today."

The man nodded. "Deer used to be great in number around here, but no longer. The deer have moved north to the mountains, where water is more plentiful."

Blaze glanced around the other side of the man, searching for more arrowheads. He was startled to see nothing where the lower half of his right leg was supposed to be. Below his knee was a smooth stump, and nothing more.

The stone worker noticed where Blaze had been looking, and said, "That is why I spend my days making weapons for the hunt. I was not much older than you, and I loved to hunt. I was young and brave and foolish, when a mountain lion taught me to respect the powers of the animal kingdom, and my own small place within it."

A mountain lion! The animal whose spirit Blaze knew was within him!

"Hello, Hartah," Stonah said as he approached.

The stone worker's rigid mouth cracked into a small smile.

"Stonah, are these your friends?"

"Yes. This is Setting Sun and this is Blaze. They are people of Sinagua, and they live at the Great Cliff."

"It is a pleasure and a privilege," Hartah said as he bowed his head slightly.

"I am taking them to our dwelling to share evening meal," Stonah said.

"Then you will be my guests as well," Hartah said. "Please accept these gifts, my friends who have journeyed so far."

The stone worker handed two shiny black arrowheads to Blaze. They were a little smaller than the one the man had been making

"Give one to your companion. They are made for deer. It is a good omen that our Father Below allowed a deer to approach you today. I believe it is a sign that you will have good fortune hunting in Hohokam land."

"Thank you," Blaze said as he took the gifts. He handed one of them to Setting Sun and excitedly ran his fingers up and down his own finely carved arrowhead. It was coated with a smooth, almost shiny finish. The arrowheads Blaze made were much rougher.

"I will see you shortly," Hartah said, resuming his work.

"This way," Stonah said. "We live along the east canal."

Stonah led Blaze and Setting Sun to a canal, which ran along the other side of the marketplace. Blaze studied the canal as they walked. It was mostly dry with a trickle of water moving along the stony bottom. Nevertheless, it was quite impressive. Back at the Great Cliff, the Sinagua people had dug new channels for the river water to reach the corn and bean crops. But the Hohokam canals were much deeper and wider, and lined with stone. How many men and how many moons were needed to construct them?

"Over there!" Stonah said, pointing to large, two-floor adobe dwelling ahead. "We live in the bottom room to the left side."

Blaze and Setting Sun followed their companion up the dusty rock-lined path to the entrance. They entered the open doorway and walked past the wooden ladder, which led to the room above, and then stepped through another doorway into Stonah's home. Blaze recognized the familiar smells of a working kitchen. Two women were busy preparing food over an open fire.

The older woman was using her right hand to slowly stir a thick broth simmering in a hanging pot. In her left arm, she held a sleeping infant. Blaze marveled at the roundness of the baby's head. The soft features on the infant's face brought a smile to his own. Maybe round heads weren't so funny looking after all.

The other woman, a younger one, was vigorously kneading a ball of hard brown dough in a large pan.

"Mother!" Stonah said.

The younger woman looked up as she continued to push the dough against the bottom of the pan.

"Mother, these are my Sinagua friends, Blaze and Setting Sun."

Without a crack of a smile, Stonah's mother nodded, and returned her attention to the bread dough at her fingertips.

"I have asked my guests to share the evening meal with us tonight. Is that okay?"

Stonah's mother fired an angry glance at the older woman, who was probably Stonah's grandmother. The gray haired woman stood expressionless, and then finally spoke.

"Of course. Travelers are always welcome in our home."

Stonah's mother nodded.

"Your father and sister have gone to lug up more pots of water. Maybe you can help them."

At that moment, a beautiful dark haired girl entered through the doorway. She was the same girl that Blaze had seen in the woods! He was speechless. Following the girl was a tall man with light skin and fine features. He glanced at Blaze but did not smile.

Blaze looked back to the girl. As their eyes met, she showed no signs of recognizing him. Didn't she remember him from earlier in the day? And who was she? Was she Stonah's sister?

Just then, another girl entered the large room. This girl had lighter skin, and eyes that looked exactly like Stonah's. *She* had to be his sister.

"Father, these are my friends," Stonah said. "They are visitors from Sinagua."

"I know where they are from," the man spoke sharply.

"Blaze, Setting Sun, this is my sister Wataha, and this is her friend Shinestah. Shinestah and her family live above us."

Shinestah. Like shining star. She must be named after a god of the night lights. Blaze liked her name.

"Father," Stonah said, "they are going to share food with us this evening."

"I don't know if that is a good idea," the man said.

"Brownwuf!" Stonah's mother said sharply. "An invitation has been made!"

"There is much going on in our village tonight. Perhaps our visitors would choose to decline. We will not be offended."

Blaze and Setting Sun exchanged puzzled glances. What was going on? Why were Stonah's mother and father so unfriendly? Did they hate flatheads like Bravegart did? Blaze glanced back towards Shinestah. She had been looking at Blaze but quickly turned her eyes aside. Blaze felt his heart skip a beat. Why was he so intrigued by her? She was only a girl.

"Maybe we will share food another time," Setting Sun finally said. "Our families must be concerned about where we are. Thank you for the invitation."

Stonah flashed an angry glance at his father, but he said nothing.

Blaze nodded in agreement and followed Setting Sun out through the doorway. Stonah followed the boys out of the room. Blaze glanced back as he was leaving, and his eyes found Shinestah's once again. This time she did not look away. Instead she smiled. Blaze smiled back as he left.

"I'm sorry," Stonah whispered once they were outside the hut. "I don't understand my father. He is always kind to travelers. It is very strange."

"That's okay," Blaze said.

"Do you still want to play guayball tomorrow?" Stonah asked Blaze and Setting Sun.

"Too rough for me," Setting Sun said.

"I would be honored," Blaze answered excitedly.

"I'll see you at early sun in the middle of the plaza. I'll take you to the field from there. It will be fun. Most of the boys my age play."

"I'll be there," Blaze answered eagerly.

CHAPTER 9

▼

Walking back to his camp, Blaze barely noticed the hustle and bustle of the crowded Hohokam settlement. Instead, all he could think about was playing guayball. He was sure that he would make his Sinagua tribe proud. He was fast and strong, and determined to play well and win. All his skills as a warrior would be put to the test, and it was a test that Blaze was sure he would pass.

While punching and catching the ball would be new to him, Blaze trusted that his speed and bravery would be enough for him to contribute. His grandfather had taught him that a battle is won first with the heart, then with the head, and finally with the hands. And his grandfather had said many times that Blaze had the heart of a great warrior.

By the time they approached their camp outside the village, the sun had already gone down. Only a trace of pink on the rocky horizon gave evidence of Father Sun's journey across the sky. Hunger pangs began to push the thought of guayball out of Blaze's mind.

"Blaze, Setting Sun!" Swift Deer called out. There was urgency in his voice.

"Father," Blaze responded, and tipped his head respectfully.

"Where have you been?"

"Hunting," Blaze answered.

"No one can hunt when Father Sun has retired. That is foolish, especially in unknown lands."

"Father, we were taken to Snaketown, and went to the home of a new friend that we met in the woods as we were hunting."

"A Hohokam boy?" Blaze's father asked suspiciously.

By this time, most of the men were surrounding Blaze and Setting Sun, eagerly listening to them.

"Yes," Blaze said. "He was Hohokam. Is that not okay?"

"No, that is fine, my young friend," Great Bear spoke out. "I am pleased that our Hohokam friends opened their doors to you."

Blaze returned a puzzled expression. Why would they not open their doors? The people of Sinagua and the people of Hohokam had been friendly for countless harvests. The quiet tension of unspoken words hung in the air.

Setting Sun's father finally broke the silence. "Boys," Tall Grass began, "there was a problem today with a band of our hunters. We killed four deer, and turned over the customary one to our Hohokam hosts. They demanded two. Blaze, your father explained that for years, when we have hunted in Hohokam land, we have offered one in four kills to our hosts. When Hohokam hunters travel to Sinagua, they do the same. Yet a tall dark man with angry eyes told us that deer had become more scarce, and that half of our kill must be given to them. The tall one was surrounded by many tribesmen, each armed with arrows and spears. They said that there would be no discussion, and just took a second deer."

"And we let them do that?" Blaze asked.

"What could we do?" Swift Deer said. "There were many more Hohokam than Sinaguas. It was essential that we keep the peace. We are not a tribe of warriors."

"Neither are the Hohokam, but they certainly acted like warriors!" Blaze argued.

"Respect your elders!" Great Bear ordered in an icy voice that commanded respect and fear.

No one spoke a word. Blaze let his eyes fall respectfully to the ground, and quietly said, "I beg your forgiveness."

Great Bear nodded, and turned away.

"Setting Sun," Tall Grass said to his son, "we feared that the Hohokam deed was an act of war, and we are all greatly relieved that you were welcomed into their village as guests."

We were not welcomed as guests by Stonah's mother and father, Blaze thought. And yet they had been allowed to leave freely.

Some of the younger men asked Blaze and Setting Sun about the main plaza of Snaketown. These were Sinagua men who had been on other journeys before, but never to the center of this Hohokam village. The boys described the marketplace and the craftsmen. They told about the canals and the sun-dried mud dwellings that were too numerous to count. And most of all, they talked about the great arenas and the game of guayball.

"While we were hunting today, we saw canals everywhere, and also some of those ball arenas," Large Rock said. "We saw a game being played, too. I agree, these Hohokam men are fierce competitors."

Sinagua men used to be fierce as well, Blaze knew. For many harvests, they had defended their fields from invading tribes while they built their dwellings in the Great Cliff. Lion Heart often said that the safety of the cliff had caused the Sinagua people to lose their skills as warriors.

"I saw a contest, too," Fleet Foot said. "It was a great spectacle." Fleet Foot, like Large Rock, had earned manhood three harvests ago, just after they went on a journey to the land of the great water. "Guayball is a game that our people would do well to learn."

Yes, thought Blaze. Fleet Foot would make a good warrior. He was one of the fiercest hunters in all of Sinagua.

"They say that the Hohokam are low on food." Spear Thrower said. "It seems unwise to waste so much energy on a game when they could be hunting or farming."

Blaze opened his mouth to argue, but stopped himself. Spear Thrower was surely trying to win favor from Great Bear and the other elders. Blaze was angry, but to argue with Spear Thrower, even though he was just a boy, was the same as arguing with the Chief Elder and the other elders. It was best to remain silent. Instead Blaze shot Spear Thrower a look of scorn while the other men talked for a while longer, sharing stories of their day. As the fire went down, the conversation dwindled until the only noise in the night was the occasional crackle from the glowing wood coals.

Laying on their blankets, Setting Sun whispered to Blaze, "Maybe playing in that game tomorrow is not a good idea."

"Of course it is," Blaze answered without thinking. He had never wanted to do anything so badly in his life. Nothing would keep him from the guayball game the next day!

"Maybe we should tell the elders what we are going to do," Setting Sun suggested.

"No," Blaze said. "We are no longer children! We can take care of ourselves. Besides, if we do not show up, it will be seen as an unfriendly gesture, and also as a sign of weakness. We know from our animal friends that the appearance of bravery is more important than bravery itself."

"You're probably right," Setting Sun said. "But still, the elders should know."

Blaze shook his head to indicate he thought otherwise. "Just bring your beads and bet on me tomorrow. You'll walk away with an abundance of riches."

A grin automatically lit up Setting Sun's face. Blaze knew exactly what to say with Setting Sun. The young Sinagua warrior smiled contentedly as he shut his eyes and began his journey to the world of dreams.

CHAPTER 10

▼

"Stonah!" Blaze called out.

The short Hohokam boy turned around and waved. Blaze and Setting Sun made their way through the crowd of people in the marketplace and approached their friend.

Blaze still could not get used to the number of people in this huge village. A city is what they called it. There were two major cities in the Hohokam world. Woven between and around those cities were numerous smaller villages, mostly about the size of Blaze's home.

In the great tapestry of the Hohokam world, most of the settlements were connected by canals. He had seen some the day before, and he knew that similar canals were everywhere. Water had always been less plentiful here than in Sinagua, and so these canals were necessary to bring the precious liquid to each village so that enough food could be grown.

"Blaze! Setting Sun! You came!"

"Why wouldn't we?" Blaze asked. "Couldn't you tell how much I wanted to play your game of guayball?"

"My mother and father told me that you might not be allowed to come. There was a hunting problem yesterday between your people and mine."

"Yes," Setting Sun said. "We were told about it. We heard that your tribesmen were demanding half of our kill instead of the usual one quarter."

"That's true," Stonah said. "Our elders struggled with that decision. There was much disagreement among them."

"Why did they do it?" Blaze asked.

"Game is growing scarce. We barely have enough food to feed our people. Ever since the generosity of the rain gods ended some harvests ago, we have not been able to grow as much corn or beans as we need, and hunting has become more important to us. Much of the deer and antelope have gone in search of more water themselves, and what is left has been hunted more heavily."

"But Stonah," Blaze argued, "for countless harvests, all the people of the earth have given one fourth of their kill to the host tribe. It is not right to change it. It can only lead to bad feelings."

"When stomachs are empty, one must do what is necessary. That's what some say. Anyway, that is the business of our elders. That is not our concern. Let's go play guayball!"

"Yes!" Blaze agreed, as he and Setting Sun followed Stonah away from the plaza.

Just beyond the main cluster of dwellings, the three boys approached an enormous egg-shaped arena with large baskets at each end. Like the one Blaze had seen the day before, this too looked like a huge, shallow bowl dug into the ground. There were two groups of boys, one on each side of the arena. Each group was punching or kicking a ball from boy to boy.

"That is my pod," Stonah said, "painted green, like me. You are both my guests, and so you two will play with me."

"I'm not playing!" Setting Sun cried. "Don't you remember? I'm just here to watch!"

"And wager, if that is done," Blaze added.

"The men always wager, but we only do sometimes."

"How do you determine which groups are enemies?"

"Not enemies," Stonah laughed. "They are our opponents. Snake-town has two pods of men. The men from the east part of our city play against those from the west. And so the boys, too, divide into an East pod and a West pod."

"Wow," Blaze muttered.

"Most villages have one guayball pod," Stonah said, "and they play against neighboring villages. Because Snaketown has so many people, we have two pods. We are from the east, and the men from east Snake-town play against pods from every other village. But of all the pods, our greatest rival is the pod made up of our friends and fellow tribes-men from the other side of our own city. Those games are the most fiercely played and highly wagered on in all of Hohokam."

Setting Sun's eyes opened wide.

"The elders spend much time talking about the great East-West games of their young manhood," Stonah continued. "A victory against a Snaketown rival will be long remembered, and brings much glory to your dwelling cluster."

Blaze wished that he was a Hohokam. At that moment, he wanted it so badly it almost hurt. Instead, he was from a people who discouraged any game playing at all.

"Don't you wear the shoulder and leg protection that the men wear?"

"No, only the men on the village pod wear pads. It is a great honor to be chosen to represent your people on a guayball pod. A young com-petitor is presented with his own pads before his first game. It is a sacred moment, as the gods each wore their special shields in the great battles of the Underworld. You see, our contests are held to honor those gods."

"Stonah!" a boy cried from the far end of the arena. "Let's go!"

"Come on," Stonah said to Blaze.

Stonah ran to join his green podmates, and Blaze followed. Setting Sun walked up to the group as well.

"Who's the flathead?" a short, heavy boy asked.

"He's a Sinagua," a boy they called Desersun said harshly. "His name is Blaze, and he will be playing with us."

"On our pod?" another boy asked.

"He is my guest," Stonah stated. "Blaze, that's Stronebul, Longarrah, Desersun and Rahwin. They are all on the East pod. Podmates, this is Blaze of the Great Cliff."

No one said a word.

"Let's show him how to play," Stonah said.

"Here!" Longarrah called out, as the tall, slender boy punched the ball to Blaze.

Blaze grabbed it with his hands.

"No!" Stronebul yelled. It was the same boy, the short, heavy one who had first called him a flathead. Blaze noticed that even though he was short, the muscles on his arms and chest gave him great size around. "You are not allowed to touch the ball with the inside of your hands! Throw it back to me!"

Blaze used his hands to throw the ball back.

"No, flathead!" Stronebul cried. "I said that you cannot touch the ball with the inside of your hands! You use your forearms to cradle the ball and then lift your arms to throw the ball up. When it comes down, use your fists to punch it forward. That is how you pass a guayball."

"Let me try," Blaze said.

"Let him, Stronebul," Stonah said.

The muscular Hohokam boy punched the ball perfectly to Blaze. This time, Blaze kept his fists closed and let the ball hit him in his chest as he trapped it there with his arms.

"Good catch, Blaze!" Stonah said.

"He should let it hit the soft underside of his forearms first, and them pull it into his chest," Stronebul said. "Otherwise, it will be difficult to catch a long throw. The chest is too hard and cannot give with the ball. It will bounce off too quickly."

Blaze nodded. He knew that the boy had meant to be critical and show him to be a fool, but he did realize that the advice was good, and would prove to be helpful if he were to master this game.

"Over here!" Stonah called to Blaze. Cradling the ball, Blaze kept both arms together and let the ball roll down his upturned forearms. Just as it reached his wrists, he gently tossed it up in the air right in front of him. He brought both fists up and popped the soft guayball toward his friend. Instead of going where he had aimed it, the ball skittered off to the left.

"Good try," Longarrah said. "But you actually punched the ball with only one of your fists. You kept your hands apart. Instead, hold them together, thumb to thumb and knuckle to knuckle. Keep them together, and let them work as one. Like this."

Longarrah demonstrated the correct hand position, then called out, "Pass me the ball."

"Longarrah, here!" Stonah called back, then punched the guayball perfectly to the boy. Blaze was amazed at how naturally they sent the smooth round object to one another.

As Longarrah lofted the ball in front of himself, preparing to punch a pass, Blaze studied the boy's arm movement. From the taut biceps and flexed shoulder muscles, Blaze could see how much force Longarrah used to push his two fists together. Pushing so hard against one another, his fists did form one surface as he raised his clenched hands to punch the ball up. And then he took all the energy keeping the fists together, and unleashed it into a powerful upward thrust. The ball sailed high into the air, landing right into the hands of Setting Sun.

"That's not how to catch!" Stronebul yelled. "Haven't you seen a thing?"

"He's not playing, Stronebul," Stonah said. "Setting Sun, give the ball to Blaze. Let him try again."

Setting Sun pushed the ball on the ground to his friend. Blaze picked it up with closed fists, and in his head stepped through the exact sequence of arm movements needed to send the ball to a podmate.

Using all his concentration, he tossed the ball a couple of arm lengths over his head. As it came down towards him, Blaze brought his clenched fists together, and pushed them hard against one another. He then popped his closed hands up to meet the ball, and sent the soft brown mass high into the air.

"Great throw!" Stonah said proudly.

Stronebul grunted and nodded to Blaze. Blaze's chest was bursting with pride while he struggled to mask his emotion. His grandfather had taught him that a great Sinagua warrior must not show his feelings towards his enemy. But Stronebul was going to be working together with him in the game. He was on the same pod! So why did he feel like an enemy?

The boys on the East Snaketown pod passed a ball back and forth, sometimes running as they were throwing or catching the ball. Blaze had figured out that they called it a pass, when the ball was punched from one boy to another. He again marveled at how the boys led the receiver of the ball by throwing ahead of where he was, just as in hunting, where you aim your arrow ahead of your running target. That was a skill at which Blaze excelled. As Blaze threw and caught passes, he did so with more and more confidence and skill. With each exchange of the ball he grew more certain that this was something he could be very good at. Just practicing, he was already feeling a great love for this game.

"Is the East ready?" a voice boomed from the other side of the arena.

The deep, clear voice sounded familiar. Blaze spotted the boy who had spoken. It was Bravegart! Bravegart looked directly at Blaze and his stonelike expression slowly broke into a smile. But it was not a smile like Stonah's or Setting Sun's. It was an angry smile. Blaze moved his eyes up and down the tall boy's hard muscular body. Suddenly, playing this game did not seem like such fun. Blaze had a feeling that the Sinaguas and Hohokam might someday be enemies, and the need for Sinagua warriors would be great. Blaze had been secretly training for that day. If it came, Bravegart would surely be a leader for the

Hohokam. Eyeing his formidable opponent, Blaze felt that this contest held great meaning for the future.

CHAPTER 11

▼

Stronebul and Bravegart stood face to face with the ball on the ground between them. The two boys held each other's shoulders as the rest of the competitors moved into position. Each pod had eight boys for this game. Stonah had said that a pod must have at least six and at most ten players. When the shadow of the sun clock touched the end stone, the game would be over.

Blaze had been told to play back at first. He would be what they called a stopper. His job was to stop the opponent from passing or carrying the ball over the endline. If someone had the ball, usually an attacker, Blaze could hit, hold or tackle him.

Blaze was scared and excited. He was scared that he might make a mistake and cost the East a point. If that happened, the other players on the pod would blame Stonah, and Blaze did not want his new friend to suffer. Blaze was also a little afraid to face Bravegart in battle, and this game would be a battle. While Blaze had always imagined himself a fearless warrior, he had never actually been put to the test. His mock fights had always been against his grandfather, and Blaze knew that his grandfather would never actually hurt him. But Bravegart was different. Bravegart would surely relish the opportunity to harm him. In fact, Blaze expected that Bravegart would go out of his way to do so.

Fear and exhilaration fought for control of Blaze's heart. This would be his first battle, and he had a lot to prove to these Hohokam, and to himself. He loved to compete at anything, and the allure of this game was unlike any other. Stonah smeared the warm, greasy paint over Blaze's shoulders and across his back and chest. As the thick, oily liquid sank into his skin, Blaze's anticipation grew even more. Finally, with his back and chest covered with green paint, he was ready.

The two pod leaders released each other's shoulders and fought for the ball at their feet. Just as Bravegart had it between his fists, Stronebul drove his left foot into the ball, kicking it along the ground deep into the arena. A red painted boy from the West let the ball roll up his foot and he flipped it up into his arms, where he cradled it and ran hard to his left.

Most of the green boys from the East headed to their right, cutting off their red opponent's direct path to the end area. Some angled in directly at the ball carrier while others lay back to intercept him further up the playing surface should he get by the first wave of attackers. Blaze was told to mostly stay back and in the middle, and that is what he did. The ball carrier, a fast runner with a completely shaven head, dropped the ball and kicked it to the opposite side of the arena.

There, all alone, Bravegart stood awaiting the pass as it fell from the sky right into his open arms. He cradled the ball tightly to his chest and sprinted up the arena. Blaze stood back with only one podmate, Desersun. Bravegart faked to the side, fooling Desersun. Suddenly, Blaze realized that Bravegart was running hard, straight at him! Bravegart was so big and so fast, Blaze stood frozen with terror. What should he do? His first instinct was to try to knock Bravegart over with a shoulder to his midsection. Or maybe he should strike with his fists, and try to inflict pain. Or perhaps he should try to pop the ball from his chest, or maybe just steer him to the side, giving other boys from the East a chance to get back and help out.

Blaze did not have time to think. Instead, he followed his instinct, and instinct told him to lay the boy flat on the ground. He ran hard towards the oncoming ball carrier, but before he could crush him with a tackle, Bravegart turned his shoulders to the left, drawing Blaze to that side. Then, Bravegart pivoted hard to run to his right, and Blaze was left grabbing at empty air as his opponent trotted easily to the center of the end line and tossed the ball ahead and through the large basket.

"Two to nothing," he called out.

"Blaze, you have to stop him!" Stronebul roared.

Stonah jogged over and quietly explained to Blaze, "When you are the last man back, don't charge too soon. Wait until *he* makes his move. Force him to the side, which will give the rest of us a chance to get back."

Blaze nodded. That made sense.

"But why did they get two points?" Blaze asked.

"If the ball goes into the basket, you earn two points. Just taking it over the line gets you only one."

Blaze nodded again as he noticed a crowd of young people on the side of the arena. They were mostly girls and younger boys, but some older boys were there as well, and even a few older men. A group of boys surrounded Setting Sun. He must be betting on the game, Blaze thought.

And then Blaze spotted Shinestah. She was looking right at him! Suddenly Blaze was even more embarrassed by his error on the field. He nodded to her and she smiled back. More determined than ever to avoid another mistake, he turned his attention back to the competition.

Moving up the arena with the ball for the East was Rahwin, their smallest boy. He was fast and quick, though. He accelerated to his right, drawing only three opponents towards him. He faked the first red boy, just as Bravegart had faked Blaze, but the other two opponents closed in from each side, giving Rahwin nowhere to run. Without looking, he quickly punched the ball to his left, where Stonah easily received the pass. How did Rahwin know that Stonah would be there?

Blaze's heart pounded with excitement. It was a beautiful pass. Blaze did notice that as soon as Rahwin had released the ball, the two boys in red had flattened him.

Blaze thought that they could only hit a boy who was carrying the ball! He would have to ask Stonah about that later.

Meanwhile, Stonah moved gracefully up the middle, with boys in red approaching from each side. Stonah sprinted to his left and then shuffled the ball to his right. Coming from behind at that exact moment was Stronebul who was speeding past Stonah and caught the pass in his arms without even slowing down. It was incredible how well these boys moved together. His grandfather had always said that a man could not be a great warrior or a great chief until he began to think as a 'we' and not as an 'I.' The players on the East pod certainly played as a 'we.' And yet the individual skill was essential as well.

Stronebul plunged through two opponents, sending them each sprawling in different directions. Suddenly only Bravegart stood between Stronebul and the end line. Blaze saw how Bravegart backpedaled as Stronebul approached. With his feet moving in a stutter-step and his hands held out in front of him, Bravegart was balanced and ready. He was prepared to move to the left or right to stop his charging opponent.

As Bravegart was taking another step backwards, Stronebul wrapped his arms tightly around the ball, dropped his left shoulder down, and drove forward. Stronebul's shoulder smashed into Bravegart's chest. The red leader's legs buckled, and he fell flat on his backside. Stronebul trampled over him, ran up to the line, and tossed the ball forward to the basket. As it dropped in, he called out, "Two to two!"

Before play started up again, Blaze asked about hitting the boy who had already made his pass. Stonah explained that once you had committed yourself to hit, it was impossible to stop, even if your man passed the ball. A player was allowed to complete a hit.

"Couldn't you flatten a kid long after a pass, and say that you could not stop?" Blaze asked.

"It would be dishonorable," Stonah said. "Winning without honor is even worse than losing."

Blaze hustled back to get in position. The boys from the West were shuffling the ball back and forth, evading the attackers from the East. Bravegart dropped the ball in front of himself as he ran, then kicked it long and high, sending it half the length of the arena. Blaze, who was the last boy back for the East, watched the ball sail over his head and hit the ground, rolling towards the end line. Out of the corner of his eye, Blaze saw a figure in red streaking by his side, flying towards the rolling ball.

Blaze pivoted, digging his sandal clad feet into the ground, and moved his legs as quickly as he could. He had always been proud of his speed. He was the fastest boy in his village, but these Hohokam seemed speedier than the boys of the Great Cliff. The boy in red was a half step ahead of Blaze, but Blaze pushed himself as hard as he could, and moved even with his opponent. Blaze felt an elbow drive into his side as they both approached the ball. The boy from the West pod leaned over, and as his fists surrounded the ball, Blaze whipped his body around in a slide, kicking the ball out of his opponent's hands. It rolled towards the side of the arena, where Longarrah scooped it up for the East and began to jog forward.

Burning pain ran up and down the whole right side of Blaze's scraped body as he struggled to push himself off the ground. Suddenly, a strong hand reached under his arm and pulled him up. It was Stronebul.

"Great job," he called as he turned his back to Blaze and sprinted towards the ball carrier.

Blaze's heart swelled with pride. He no longer noticed the pain. Instead he felt more alive than ever. At that moment, Blaze knew that his destiny was to be a warrior.

The game continued, with both teams scoring a number of points. As the shadow approached the end of game stone, the score was tied 9-9. Blaze was exhausted. He was banged and scraped and bruised, and every muscle in his body ached, but he had played a good game. While he was not yet skilled at passing or catching the ball, his speed and quickness had helped him stop many of the West pod's attackers from scoring. Blaze had decided that he did not care how hurt he became. All that mattered was stopping Bravegart and his West pod. The other boys from the East had begun to rally around Blaze, making him feel every bit as important to the pod as anyone else. He was part of the 'we' of the East.

Blaze was standing in the middle of the arena when Rahwin kicked a long pass perfectly to Stonah. Stonah was sprinting past the last red-painted boy when the ball landed in his arms and he skipped over the end line.

"Ten to nine!" he called out.

"Stop them here!" Stronebul commanded. There would be time for just one more run up the arena for the West. Blaze and his podmates from the East had to stop the boys in red.

After four quick passes, the West had the ball in the center of the arena. Blaze and Stronebul were at the rear, backing up the East's two mid-arena players. Four red attackers approached, passing the ball skillfully to one another, avoiding each charging boy in green. And then Bravegart had the ball. One podmate was running at his side. He faked to his right and passed the ball to the boy on his left. Stronebul had guessed he would do that, and dove to intercept the pass, but his outstretched arms were not long enough. His fingertips barely grazed the rough brown ball, which was caught and instantly sent back to Bravegart. Blaze was alone, the last green boy back, facing the two charging boys in red. If he went for Bravegart, his opponent would surely shuffle off a pass to his podmate for an easy score. Otherwise, Bravegart himself would walk in for the score.

Blaze decided to play Bravegart, and at least force him to make the pass. He backed off, waiting to see which way his powerful foe would go. Blaze hoped that Bravegart would try to score himself. Was the West pod leader an 'I' or a 'we?'

Blaze would not be fooled so easily by a fake this time. Charging forward, Bravegart threw a shoulder to his left. Blaze held his ground. A moment later, Bravegart slammed into Blaze, butting his head into Blaze's stomach. Blaze felt the air forced painfully from his chest, as Bravegart trampled over his falling body. With all his strength, Blaze reached up and grabbed Bravegart's foot, bringing his body down. The ball rolled free, and suddenly Blaze's podmate Stronebul was scooping it up as two West attackers charged. Stronebul booted the ball nearly the length of the arena! As it rolled on the sandy surface, the young people by the sun clock raised their hands, indicating that the contest was over. The East had won!

All eight of the green painted boys came together and patted each other on the back in celebration. No one said a word about any individual's contributions. The pod had been victorious, and each of the eight boys had given their all in the effort.

Blaze looked to the side of the arena and saw Shinestah beaming with joy. She nodded slightly to Blaze, and then turned around, talking to the cluster of girls next to her. Blaze wanted to talk to her, too, but he knew that he should remain with his pod.

His attention returned to the arena as all the boys from each pod lined up at the center, facing the line of their opponents. They all nodded towards their foes and mumbled a short chant of thanks to the gods of the Lower World, whose battles they had respectfully recreated. The anger seemed to be gone. All of the boys in red who had fought so hard against Blaze during the game now greeted him with respect. Except Bravegart. When Blaze's eyes met those dark eyes of the fierce boy-warrior, Blaze almost had to turn away. Waves of pure hatred radiated from Bravegart. Blaze knew that not only had he defeated the proud fighter, but he had also forced Bravegart to make an unforgivable mistake. Bravegart could have easily won the contest with a pass to his podmate, but the competition had become personal to him. He had tried to teach the flathead a lesson and personally beat Blaze one-against-one. He had played as an 'I' and not as a 'we.' Bravegart had not only lost the game, but he had lost the respect of every contestant and every observer at that arena. Bravegart seethed with anger. Blaze sensed that Bravegart would make someone pay. Something told Blaze that he had won a battle today, but a war had begun. He feared this victory might be one that he would regret.

CHAPTER 12

▼

"Yes, you fattened my pouch," Setting Sun said, patting his blue woven bag.

Blaze smiled as he heard the familiar jingle of beads in Setting Sun's treasure pouch.

"I am glad to be of service, my friend," Blaze said.

"I got quite good odds on the competition," Setting Sun said, "thanks to our friend Shinestah."

Setting Sun nodded to Shinestah. Blaze smiled back towards her, but blushed when their eyes met.

"Yes," Setting Sun continued, "she convinced those Hohokam boys that a pod with a flathead could never overcome the mighty West Village."

Flathead? Shinestah thought of him as a flathead? A wave of sadness ran over him. He worked hard to keep the smile on his face, but his eyes could not hide the hurt he felt inside.

Shinestah tilted her head and looked to Blaze with puzzled eyes, then seemed to understand. She quickly said, "Blaze, I knew that you would make yourself and your people of the Great Cliff proud."

The kindness in her voice soothed his spirit.

"Yes," Setting Sun said. "Thanks to Shinestah, the young boys from the West Village put up three beads to each one of mine. Of course,

Shinestah, I can barely carry my treasure back to our camp because of you."

Shinestah laughed. Her laughter had the sound of beautiful music to Blaze. He looked at her again, his hurt feelings almost gone.

Seeming to read his mind, Shinestah gently stroked Blaze's hair and quietly said, "I think that Sinaguas have beautifully shaped heads."

Blaze could not say a word in return. All thoughts of the contest and of Bravegart had flown from his mind. Her touch had taken his breath away.

"You competed well, my friend," Stonah said to Blaze, putting an arm around his shoulder. "Of course, your skill at catching and throwing the ball does need some improvement."

Blaze smiled. He had managed to drop a number of high passes, and his punches were not too accurate, but he had always been sure to kick any stray balls far out of the danger area near the East end line. He had strong legs for kicking, and could run as fast as any of the boys on either pod. Lion Heart had told him that his own father and his father's father had been the fastest men in all of Sinagua. The gift of swift feet had been passed down from father to son in his bloodline, and that had helped him defend his end line in his game of guayball. Still, Blaze yearned to throw perfect passes as so many of the Hohokam boys had done.

"You know," Stonah said, "we do not often defeat the powerful pod from the West Village. It is a moment we will long treasure. Your speed and your heart were an important part of our victory. In thanks, I would like to present this ball to you."

Stonah handed Blaze a soft, round guayball, similar to he one that they had played with on the arena.

Blaze was speechless as he received the gift. He ran his fingers up and down the rough, well-worn surface, and pushed it in with his thumbs, feeling the air trapped within.

"To what great creatures do we owe thanks for this ball?" Blaze asked.

"The outer layers are made from the fibers of the guayule plant. The inner part of guayballs are usually made of soft plants like cotton, and some have the bladder of an animal, like mule or ox or buffalo, but this ball is special. Inside this is the bladder of a mountain lion."

A mountain lion! Blaze's heart skipped a beat.

"The bladder was filled with air, and sewn shut and sealed with pitch, lined with guayule fiber, and then sewn inside the woven guayule husk."

"A mountain lion!" Blaze uttered out loud.

"Yes, this is a most special ball."

"I cannot accept this gift. It must mean so much to you, my friend Stonah."

"Take it," Shinestah said. "It would not be his without your brave play. Stonah just won it."

"From Bravegart!" Setting Sun added.

"What?" Blaze said.

"Yes," Setting Sun said proudly, "that foolish Bravegart wagered a guayball with a mountain lion sac against Stonah's beads. He was so sure that his pod would win!"

Bravegart's ball? A shudder of excitement and fear ran through Blaze. No wonder Bravegart had been so angry.

"Why don't you come tomorrow, Blaze," Stonah said, "and I can teach you more of the art of throwing and catching. The boys of the East Village pod would be proud to have you play and learn with us."

"I would love to," Blaze said excitedly.

"And if you stay for the evening, you can see a Grand Sacrifice on the Great Plaza."

"Grand Sacrifice?"

"We offer blood to the Great Gods."

Blood? Someone is killed to please the gods? Blaze had heard of such rituals.

Stonah seemed to notice the look of concern on Blaze's face and added, "An animal is killed, and then a boy-man is chosen to be marked."

"Marked?"

"When a Hohokam boy becomes a man, his chest is cut with a distinctive mark. It is a great ceremony with beautiful costumes and great dancing. You must come."

"I shall ask my elders," Blaze answered.

"Everyone in all of Snaketown will be there," Stonah said. "East and West are one."

Everyone will be there? Blaze tightened his grip on his guayball. He would rather not see Bravegart, but how could he honorably refuse this invitation? On the other hand, Shinestah would be there. Blaze shuddered. Great conflict loomed on the horizon.

CHAPTER 13

▼

"Blaze! Setting Sun! You're all right!" Running Stream cried, sounding relieved, as he ran out from the camp to greet the two boys. "Blaze, why are you painted?"

"I'll explain," Blaze answered, not wanting to tell the boy the whole story at that moment.

'Boy,' Blaze thought, turning that word over in his mind. He still thought of Running Stream as a boy, even though two harvests ago he had earned manhood. Running Stream, like Blaze, had always wanted to be a warrior, and sometimes still secretly practiced fighting with Blaze.

Blaze saw all his people there at the camp. Strange, Blaze thought. Some of them should be hunting right now.

Swift Deer stepped up to greet Blaze and Setting Sun. Blaze bowed respectfully to his father, and Setting Sun did the same.

"We are going home," Swift Deer stated flatly.

"Home?" Blaze asked. "But our journey has just begun! I still need to see Prongah to get medicines!"

"It has been decided, my son."

"But Father, I have not earned my first kill!"

"There is ample time for that later. We must leave immediately."

"But why?"

Swift Deer turned his eyes towards Running Stream, whose head hung in shame.

"Running Stream chose to act without the approval of the journey elders," Swift Deer answered. "He stole back the disputed deer from the Hohokam. Three Hohokam men caught him and were bringing him back to their village when we saw them."

"So they just let him go?" Blaze asked.

"No," Blaze's father said. "Only after facing our six drawn bows did they release him. One of the Hohokam men was prepared to fight, even in the face of certain death. But the two others convinced him that it was wiser to let Running Stream go."

"That man, Father, the one who wanted to fight. Do you know his name?"

"Yes. They called him Greatgart."

Greatgart! An icy chill crept up Blaze's spine. Blaze remembered the man's skill and fearlessness in the arena. He also thought of the anger and hatred in Greatgart's son, Bravegart.

"Greatgart vowed revenge as we left."

"Why didn't you kill him, Father?"

"Your father acted wisely," said Great Bear, the journey's chief elder. "Had we slain those Hohokam men, war would surely have broken out. We have been at peace for three generations, and are not prepared for war. It was wiser to let those men go."

"May I speak my mind, Chief Elder?" Blaze asked. He knew that it was not acceptable for a boy to question the actions of any elder.

"You may," Great Bear said.

"I fear that letting Greatgart go was unwise. Greatgart is one of their fiercest warriors. He is their strongest and most skilled in battle, and if he is like his son, he has an angry heart and will seek a reason to kill."

"How do you know such a thing?"

Blaze was forced to tell Great Bear and all the elders about playing guayball with Stonah's pod. Swift Deer flashed Blaze a look of disappointment. Blaze told everything about the previous two days, everything except about Shinestah. That did not seem important to relate.

The elders stood pondering all they had heard, while the young men passed around Blaze's guayball, smelling it and squeezing it.

"Your knowledge is very useful, young Blaze," Lion Heart finally said. "Our decision to leave was clearly a wise one. And our decision to release the three Hohokam men was wise as well."

Blaze raised his eyebrows in a questioning manner.

"Had we killed those three warriors, they would have instantly sent a party out to kill us in revenge. There are many more Hohokam than Sinaguas, and certainly many more than we have in our party. They are prepared for quick travel and we are not. They are prepared for battle and we are not. Had we killed the three captors of Running Stream, we would be preparing for our journey to the Great Underground at this moment."

"Great Bear," Blaze asked, his mind still struggling to understand their situation, "might they come after us anyway, after what Running Stream did, and after we rescued him?"

"Yes, they might."

"And so wouldn't we be better off without them having Greatgart?"

Great Bear paused and calmly explained. "With or without Greatgart, they would greatly outnumber us. He is not important. But had we killed their three tribesmen, they surely would have decided to attack us. Now, there is a chance they might not come after us. After all, they did get their deer back. We let them keep it after we had taken back Running Stream. Also, attacking us is no longer an obvious course of action. Like our elders, theirs surely are a mix of different ideas and viewpoints. Should they choose to pursue us, it would be after much deliberation. By that time, we would have a good head start. Moving quickly, we should be able to get back to the Great Cliff before they catch up to us."

"But Great Bear," Setting Sun asked. "How will we defend ourselves if the Hohokam are so numerous? They have more people living today in one city than we have had in all the harvests put together at the Great Cliff!"

"We live at the Great Cliff because we are so few, Setting Sun. We built it so that a handful of people could defend it against much greater numbers. That is why we have not needed to pursue the art of war. The women and grand elders themselves could fight off an enemy of young warriors. Our doors are so small, that even if they could get up our ladders, they would not be able to get in. The slightest poke with a great pole would send any intruder plunging to his passage to the Great Underground."

Blaze noticed that most of the men in the traveling party were busy packing their belongings. He nodded to Great Bear in appreciation for taking the time to explain things so well. He hoped that some day he might have as much wisdom as his Chief Elder. Blaze suddenly felt guilty about the many times he had thought of Great Bear as a fearful old man.

As Blaze collected his few belongings, he remembered that he was supposed to see Stonah the next day. What will his Hohokam friend think when he does not show up? With sadness, Blaze carefully put his guayball, Bravegart's ball, into his traveling pouch.

And then the image of Shinestah appeared in the eye of his mind. What would she think when he did not show up? A dull ache tugged at his heart as he prepared for his journey back to the Great Cliff.

CHAPTER 14

▼

One foot in front of another, Blaze pushed on. They said that he could not make it back to the Great Cliff before dark. He would show them.

Blaze dropped his carry-bag and held his fist out at arm's length in front of him. Aligning the lower edge with the horizon, he placed the fist of his other hand above. The top edge of his upper fist almost reached the sun. In familiar territory, Blaze knew that he could normally run back to the Great Cliff with two fists of sky remaining for the sun to drop, but he had been running since high sun and had little strength left in his legs. Still, Blaze was sure that if he could make it home, then his animal spirit would appear to him. That was the reason he had gone on ahead of his fellow journeyers.

It was difficult to keep going. His spirits were low after such a disappointing journey. Nothing had happened as he had planned. Blaze had hoped for both his first big game kill and his animal spirit. Why had the Great Spirit not helped him? With so many of the young men, both had happened to them on their first journey. But Blaze would return from his journey as he had started—no closer to manhood. He had even left Hohokam before seeing Prongah for medicines. Desert Cloud would be disappointed.

Blaze guessed that he would never return to Hohokam land to compete on their guayball arenas. Stonah must be wondering why Blaze never showed up. And then there was Shinestah. He might never see her again. Did she think that he did not care? He found that his mind could not erase the image of her face.

Maybe that was why Blaze's animal spirit had not come to him. With the spirit of Shinestah so filling his heart, there might not be room for his animal spirit. Or maybe it was because the Great Spirit did not approve of his secret training to be a warrior.

Still, Blaze did not want to spend his life growing corn and squash. He knew that his spirit was meant for other, greater things. His grandfather had told him that too. His grandfather believed that the Sinagua people must not lose the art of war, and Lion Heart was a respected grand elder. The Great Spirit had sent his animal spirit to him when he was young, and so the Great Spirit must respect Sinagua warriors. But why did the rest of the village elders object so to any training for war? Were they afraid? Did the Sinagua people lack the courage to fight?

"Why was I not born a Hohokam instead of a foolish flathead?" Blaze said to himself. He spit out the word *flathead* with disgust. Disgust for his people and disgust for himself.

But hearing that word, and the way he had said it, Blaze was struck with a pang of guilt. The Sinaguas were his people. He did love them, and he had always done everything he could to enter the Sinagua manhood.

"Great Spirit, I am sorry," Blaze said out loud. The Great Spirit was everywhere. Would the powerful god forgive him?

Blaze's eyes searched the world around him. The Great Spirit was in the rocks and in the sand and in the clusters of brush spotting the dry landscape. And then Blaze's eyes were drawn to a movement behind the saltbrush to his right. In a flash, a full-grown pronghorn antelope appeared. The massive beast raced around a low cliff and disappeared again.

Blaze held on to his bow and grabbed an arrow from his quiver. He sprinted towards the spot where the large animal had gone. As he stepped past the bush where he had first seen the antelope, his eyes were drawn to a motionless animal shape nestled in a crevice of the rocky red cliff above.

Blaze knew instantly that the animal on the cliff was not the antelope. What was it? The perched shape was mostly hidden in the shadows of the rock. As Blaze's eyes adjusted to the shadows of the cliff, he studied what he could make out of the brown beast. And then suddenly, he knew what is was.

It was a mountain lion! Both Blaze and the lion stared deeply into the eyes of the other. The mountain lion did not move, but its intense green eyes seemed to peer straight into Blaze's soul.

And then Blaze noticed the muscles of its hind legs slowly contract. The hump on its upper back rose as its short brown body hair seemed to stand upright. The lion was preparing to move. To attack! Very slowly, Blaze slipped an arrow onto his bow and drew it back, carefully aiming at the chest of this great creature.

The mountain lion did not move. Blaze did not move. In one leap, the great mountain lion could spring from the cliff and rip into him before he could re-aim his arrow. If the lion sprang at him and he fired, the arrow would surely land behind the lunging beast, and the lion would be upon him. Blaze wondered if he should aim up higher, and shoot to where the lion would be on its flight from the cliff? Blaze had never hunted a mountain lion before. He had only seen one other in his life, and that had been from a great distance. From his hunting experience, Blaze knew how quickly rabbits and prairie dogs moved, and he could aim with his arrow accordingly. But the mountain lion was a mystery. If Blaze wanted to kill it in mid-attack, he could only guess where to shoot.

Blaze kept his eyes glued to the eyes of the beautiful creature. He realized that if he fired his arrow at that moment, before the mountain lion began its attack, his arrow would surely strike the great beast. Would one arrow be enough to kill it? He was not sure, but he knew that if he fired it, he could drive his arrow deep within the chest of this creature.

With his life on the line, Blaze tightened his grip on his bow, but he could not release the arrow. Instead, he remained frozen, his unblinking eyes glued to the cool, eerie eyes of the powerful beast. The lion's perfectly sculpted face did not move. Reflecting a trace of sunlight, its white whiskers almost glowed next to its black nose. The line of short black hair running between its eyes looked like the war paint of ancient tribes. Its shiny brown coat of fur revealed a dark undercoat at the bent joints of its legs. Its huge paws seemed both powerful and gentle. This was truly the most magnificent and fearsome creature Blaze had ever seen. What a kill this would be! Only one other living Sinagua tribesman had ever successfully hunted a mountain lion before. Swift Arrow, a grand elder, had killed one on a journey many harvests ago. Claw marks still adorned his chest as proof of his struggle. Swift Arrow's first shot had landed in the shoulder and not the chest. The mountain lion had made him pay for that slight error.

Blaze trusted his skill with the arrow. From his position below, he was certain that he could hit the lion square in the heart. It would be a great feat on his journey to manhood. And a good shot might also save his life.

If he did not fire, Blaze knew that the mountain lion could kill him in an instant. And yet he was not afraid. Instead, an inexplicable feeling of calm came over him. He was sure that the lion understood that they each held the power to kill the other. The lion knew that Blaze could release the fatal arrow. The lion also knew that Blaze would be easy prey should it choose to attack first.

Blaze felt a power that he had never even imagined. It was not that he held the life of this mountain lion in his hands. It was more that he was one with the lion. They were equals. And the great mountain lion was acknowledging Blaze as an equal. At that moment, Blaze knew that he would not release his arrow. Instead, he remained motionless and continued to hold the stare of the lion as an understanding passed between them.

At that moment, Blaze was sure that when this creature died, its spirit would find its way to him. Had he killed the lion, its spirit would be lost to him forever. But now he knew its spirit was his. He was one with this great hunter. And yet, he did not dare to lower his weapon. How long would they remain like this?

Suddenly, his attention was drawn to another movement, this one from a brush to his side. Blaze instinctively glanced to his left and recognized the familiar curved horns of the pronghorn antelope rising above the brownish green leaves of a cat claw shrub. Was it the same antelope as before? A moment later, three more of the enormous animals were standing next to the other antelope in the open land ahead. Instantly, Blaze turned his bow and arrow towards the giant beasts. They suddenly changed direction and started to run. Instinctively, Blaze aimed his arrow a length ahead of the first stampeding animal and fired. The arrow landed right in the midsection of the beast. Blaze had led it perfectly! The giant antelope stumbled, then tumbled forward, crashing to the ground in a cloud of dust.

At that moment, Blaze remembered the mountain lion. He whipped his body around to face the cliff but the lion was gone. He searched high and low, but there was no sign of the creature.

Blaze turned back to the antelope and saw that three of them were gone, leaving only the wounded one lying before him. Blaze approached the beast, and saw that his arrow had struck the center of the creature's chest, square in the heart. In fifty shots, he could not fire one so perfectly. It usually took two or three arrows to take down an adult antelope, but one shot will suffice if it is a perfect one. And then Blaze understood. He had not acted alone in this kill. The greatest hunter of them all, the mountain lion, had helped direct his shot.

As the antelope uttered its final breath, Blaze lay his hand on the giant animal's head, and whispered thanks to the God of the Wild. He prayed for the antelope's safe passage to the Great Underworld, and thanked the creature for the gift of its spirit and flesh. He bowed his head quickly, grabbed the knife from his belt, and began to chisel away at a horn. Each horn was almost as big as one of Blaze's arms! They would make great trophies from his first large game kill.

When he had finally removed both of the curved horns, Blaze held them tightly, trying to draw on the strength of the great animal he had felled. Maybe this would enable him to run even harder in his quest for his animal spirit. Blaze then realized that there was little light remaining for him to continue his run back to the Great Cliff. If he wanted to go on, he would have to travel after dark, leaving the antelope where it was. Blaze thought about that and decided that there was no reason to continue his journey home right then. The only reason he had gone ahead was to try to see his animal spirit. He now knew, though, that no matter how long or hard he might run, his animal spirit was not ready to come to him. He had stood eye to eye with the living spirit that would be part of him one day, and he would have to wait until it left its powerful earthly body.

With calm and certainty, he sat next to the dehorned antelope, and awaited the rest of his fellow travelers. They should catch up to him by high sun the next day. Meanwhile, Blaze would have to pack the wound with dirt and cover the blood on the ground as well. He did not want the vultures and other scavengers to steal his kill. This creature would feed his people well, and from its hide, a beautiful covering would be made for his manhood ceremony. Blaze felt good.

CHAPTER 15

▼

Flying up the final rungs of the ladder with the guayball in his right hand, Blaze felt his friend below drawing closer. He was desperate to stay ahead, but it was hard to climb any faster with only one hand to use.

"I get you and it's my ball for the night!" Spear Thrower called up from just an arm's length below Blaze.

Blaze tucked the ball between his neck and his chest and used both hands to pull himself up the woven rungs to the fourth floor. As he glanced up to the ledge, the ball dropped from under his chin. Blaze automatically grabbed for it with both hands and suddenly felt himself falling backwards!

"No!" Blaze cried as he desperately lunged for the ladder, but his hand grabbed nothing but empty air. He was falling down the cliff!

At that instant a hand grabbed his ankle. His leg felt as if it were almost pulled out of its socket at the hip! He was hanging upside down, in midair, held only by one hand of Spear Thrower. Please hang on, Blaze prayed.

Looking down, Blaze saw Rattle Bone and Hard Shell appear on the ledge below. They were followed by their grandchildren, Tiger Eyes and Bear Tongue. Hanging there, upside down and helpless, Blaze burned with humiliation. His embarrassment bothered him even more than his fear of being dropped.

"Children, move!" Rattle Bone ordered, pushing the young ones inside and out of the path of a possible fall.

Golden Eagle appeared next, followed by Greenleaf and her children, Desert Fox and Green Thorn. Tiger Eyes and Bear Tongue popped their heads out of their dwelling door and also stared at Blaze who was still hanging by his ankle.

Blaze frantically reached down and finally grabbed the ladder with both hands.

"I have it," he called to Spear Thrower. "Pull me up. Slowly."

"You're too heavy. I can barely hold on to you. Try pushing yourself up the ladder."

"Okay," Blaze said, "but you pull, too!"

Spear Thrower pulled hard while Blaze, hanging upside down, used his hands and arms to push himself up the ladder.

By this time, everyone at the Great Cliff was outside, looking up or down to see what had happened. Blaze pushed his way up to the fourth floor ledge, and was greeted by the furious eyes of his mother. In her anger, she was speechless. His grandfather and older sister stood by Lightfoot's side. Coyote Claw, Black Rabbit and all their children stood behind, staring at Blaze.

"What were you doing?" Lion Heart asked angrily.

Blaze said nothing.

"Speak up!"

Blaze had never heard that tone of voice from his grandfather.

"Playing," Blaze finally whispered.

"Playing on the ladder?" Lion Heart asked in disbelief.

Blaze nodded.

"Get inside!"

Blaze realized that the rest of the people had returned to their dwellings. He trudged through the central room of Coyote Claw's family and continued on into his own home. As he stepped inside, he noticed that his mother's whole body was shaking.

"Playing on the ladder?" she asked, still almost in shock.

His face dark with shame, Blaze nodded. "I'm sorry."

"He's all right," Lion Heart said. "Let us go on. He has learned a lesson."

Blaze sat with his back against the hard stone wall and stared at the ground. Through the corner of his eye, he noticed Lightfoot and Bay Leaf continue their dinner preparations. And then Spear Thrower appeared at the entrance to their dwelling and rolled the guayball his way.

"Were you playing with *that*?" Lightfoot asked, saying *that* as if it were the Spirit of Evil itself.

Blaze said nothing. He had almost died to stop his guayball from dropping, and that was because of a foolish game he had been playing with Spear Thrower. Spear Thrower, playing a game. Who would have thought it a moon ago? Guayball had changed a lot of things. Still, Blaze did not understand how he could be so careless. He knew how important ladder safety was, and yet all he had thought about was not getting tagged by Spear Thrower, and not dropping the ball.

The smell of fried squash was beginning to divert Blaze's thoughts from his embarrassing near-accident when Swift Deer's voice rang out, calling his ascent to the fourth floor.

As Blaze's father entered the dwelling with his usual sigh, no one was talking.

"Something smells great!" he said.

Again, not a word was spoken. No one even looked at Swift Deer.

"Is something wrong?" he asked suspiciously.

"Blaze almost fell off the cliff playing guayball on the ladder," Bay Leaf said.

"I wasn't playing *guayball* on the ladder!"

"Blaze, were you playing on the ladder?" Swift Deer asked.

Blaze nodded.

"And are you hurt?"

Blaze shook his head.

"Then let us go on with the meal. I can hear the details of the near fall later. There is no need to ruin a good meal with talk of it now."

Relief washed over Blaze. He knew that his father would be angry later, but later was always better than sooner.

"Blaze, scoop up your little sister and bring her over to eat," Lightfoot said.

Blaze saw that his sister was very busy doing something in the corner of the room. And then he realized what it was.

"Chittanberry!" Blaze called. "Stop it!"

The baby ignored the yell of her brother and continued chewing the dirty brown guayball. Blaze jumped up and ran to her. He yanked the ball away from her mouth and out of her arms.

"Stop!" Blaze yelled. "You'll ruin it!"

"Blaze," Lightfoot said, "she hardly has any teeth. The soft guayule fiber is gentle on her sore gums. Her infant teeth are just starting to break through."

"And besides, she won't hurt it any more than it was hurt when you dropped it four floors down the cliff," Bay Leaf said.

"Enough arguing!" Swift Deer said. "You are behaving like children."

We *are* children, Blaze thought, but he did not dare say that to his father, especially after acting like such a child with Spear Thrower. Instead, Blaze nodded politely. He wondered how long it would be until the spirit of his mountain lion came to him. At least he was halfway to his manhood. The killing of the antelope had earned him great praise from all the people of his tribe. Even Swift Deer had been proud of him. He was so proud that he had not said a word about guayball in the half moon since they had returned from the journey. The whole tribe had feasted on antelope meat thanks to Blaze.

With that meat now gone, would his father forget about his kill and object once more to the playing of guayball? He might, especially after hearing about the accident with the guayball on the ladder. Blaze was turning the ball over in his hand when his fingers ran over a warm gooey wetness.

It was from Chittanberry's mouth! The baby had spit all over his mountain lion ball!

"She drooled all over it!" Blaze said to his mother. And it wasn't just any ball. This was Bravegart's guayball!

"The infant drool is a special wetness and only good can come of it," Lightfoot said calmly and without a trace of humor.

"So give it back to Chittanberry," Bay Leaf said, smiling.

"Chittanberry would not be chewing the ball if the cornbread you made was edible," Blaze said to his sister.

"Enough!" Light Foot commanded. "I cannot believe that you are nearly a woman, Bay Leaf, and yet you still act so much like a child. I shall have to have a conversation with your painted lady."

"Good idea," Blaze said.

"And you," Lightfoot said to Blaze, "no wonder your animal spirit does not come to you. Listen to you!"

She was right, Blaze thought. Why was it that when he was with his older sister, especially at evening meal time, he acted like he was about eight harvests old? He would try harder to behave as a Sinagua man and not as a child.

Blaze put down his guayball, then picked up his little sister and carried her over to the eating mat. He placed Chittanberry next to his mother, and sat down at his usual place.

"I hear that even Spear Thrower is playing that game of yours," Swift Deer said to Blaze.

Blaze had begun to take a bite of the corn bread when his appetite suddenly vanished.

"That boy used to have sense," Swift Deer added.

"If the Hohokam come, maybe he'll be better off with a little more fight in him," Lion Heart said.

"Father," Lightfoot quickly said to Lion Heart, "and Swift Deer, please have some more squash and beans."

Blaze noticed that his mother always tried to change the subject when her husband and her father were disagreeing with each other, and the topic was always the same. As he wiped away the last of the drool from the guayball, Blaze thought about what his mother had said. Maybe the drool *would* bring him luck. With a big guayball game set for the next day, maybe he should give his ball back to his little sister.

While Lightfoot was feeding Chittanberry, Blaze and the rest of his family all ate quietly. Blaze's mind roamed back to thoughts of guayball. A great rivalry had begun to develop between the boys and young men of the upper cliff, and those from the lower three floors. At first Spear Thrower had wanted no part of guayball, but Blaze had convinced him that as a fellow fourth floor boy, he needed to do his part. Spear Thrower had finally agreed to try the game. He had good instincts, and quickly earned the respect of the other boys. Blaze was sure that Spear Thrower was growing to love guayball. But why had they played that foolish chase game on the way back home? That might ruin everything.

As they ate, Blaze hardly noticed the taste of the food, and he even began to forget about his fall on the ladder. Only one thing remained on his mind. Playing guayball.

CHAPTER 16

▼

Blaze cradled the ball in his arms and turned his shoulder into Running Stream. This time, Running Stream did not lunge for the ball. Instead, he stood his ground with his feet planted firmly and his open arms held low. Just as Blaze leaned into his opponent, Running Stream lowered his shoulders. Instead of ramming Running Stream's upper body, Blaze thrust his shoulder into empty air. From below, Running Stream wrapped his long arms around Blaze's legs, nearly flipping him over. Blaze's arms automatically went out to break his fall against the hard, sandy ground, causing the ball to roll free. As it came to a stop, Setting Sun picked it up with his fists and raised it above his shoulders, letting it roll down his forearms into the crook of his elbows. He wrapped his arms firmly around the ball, and ran with it.

"Go!" Running Stream yelled to his lower cliff podmate.

"Stop him, Long Horn," Blaze silently mouthed as he freed himself from Running Stream's grasp.

Blaze's podmate set his feet firmly in the ground and squared off against his approaching foe, Setting Sun. He bent his knees close to the ground and held his hands in front of him, exactly as Running Stream had done. As Long Horn prepared for the impact, Setting Sun cut left and ran by his bigger and stronger opponent. Setting Sun danced to the endline and tossed the ball into the basket, raising his hands in celebration.

"We won!" Setting Sun cried.

"Great move, podmate!" Running Stream called out.

It was a good move, Blaze thought to himself. A move which I taught him. And to think that Setting Sun had wanted no part of guayball! While Blaze's slim friend was not strong, he was fast, and very smart, and had become quite a skilled passer.

While Blaze cursed his good instruction, which had turned against him, he was also pleased that Setting Sun had taken so well to this game. Blaze had wanted enough of the older boys and younger men to compete to be able to play a four-against-four contest. Without Setting Sun, they only had seven. Blaze did not want the really young boys to play with him. He wanted it to be as similar as possible to the Hohokam contest he had competed in.

Three of the older boys who had recently achieved manhood had been interested in guayball. And there were four other boys around Blaze's age or a couple of harvests younger.

"Pay up, my friend," Setting Sun said to Blaze.

Blaze remembered that he had staked an arrowhead on the game. During the contest, Blaze had not given that wager a second thought. All that had mattered was winning, being the best. But the only way that Blaze had been able to coax his friend to play was by letting him bet on the outcome.

What a foolish thing, to lose an arrowhead, Blaze thought. He would never have wagered such a precious item, except that he had been sure that the lower cliff pod could not win. He had been wrong. He had underestimated the speed and skill of Setting Sun, and the competitive spirit of Running Stream.

"At the cliff, you may choose one," Blaze said to Setting Sun. "You competed well, my friend."

"As did you," Setting Sun said, "even if you did wager poorly. Beads for an arrow head! You would never make such a trade. Why would you wager thus?"

Blaze was silent.

"It's because you were sure that you would win," Setting Sun teased his friend. "You need to bet with your head, and not with your heart. I shall instruct you in the art of betting to repay you for your guayball lessons."

"Which were well learned," Running Stream added.

Blaze said nothing, but he did smile. He needed no lessons in gambling. He had no interest in it, and still believed it to be a waste of time. But he had promised Setting Sun that he would wager on these games. And the Hohokam considered a small wager almost necessary for a contest.

"Maybe you should respect my betting instincts more," Setting Sun said.

"But your instincts said that my animal spirit would come to me on our journey," Blaze argued.

"True, I did think it would."

"And you were wrong!" Blaze proclaimed.

"I thought it would," Setting Sun replied, "but I was not sure enough to wager on it, was I?"

Blaze was silent. His friend was right. He would never beat Setting Sun at gambling. Guayball, though, was a different story.

"We have each won at guayball once," Blaze said, changing the topic. "Tomorrow, shall we have the deciding competition?"

"Not tomorrow," Spear Thrower said to his podmate. "We will all be expected to help prepare for tomorrow night's rain dance. The Rain Spirits have been called to our tribe in this time of great need."

"The next day, then," Blaze said.

Running Stream nodded in agreement. Blaze could tell by the fire in his eyes that Running Stream loved this guayball as much as anyone did. His skill had improved tremendously from playing each day.

Blaze was so glad that the last of the cotton had been picked. Now they could play guayball all the time. Blaze had picked along with Setting Sun. Not loving any part of working the land, Blaze enjoyed this activity enough because he could imagine the beautiful garments that would be spun from the product of his labor. His fingers had gone through that painful blistery stage caused by picking out countless seeds from the fiber. Blaze's fingers could move faster than Setting Sun's, but Setting Sun liked this job because he could wager on how many pots of seeds each could remove. Of course, Setting Sun knew that Blaze would always remove more, and so the bet was on how many more pots that Blaze could fill.

To Blaze, it seemed that Setting Sun had an advantage in being slower. On the other hand, Blaze enjoyed any competition, and these small contests with Setting Sun did make the task go by more quickly. Blaze never wagered anything important like his arrows, but usually bet for just beads or feathers.

The harvest had been small the past season. Another thirteen moons of scarce rain had made it more and more difficult to bring enough water to the crops. They had channeled water from the creek, but that could be stretched only so far. They had let a number of fields die, making sure that those which they did tend would produce in ample quantity.

Because of the meager harvest, the elders had allowed the men and even some boys to hunt more often. Some of the younger boys were encouraged to hunt the smaller game, like squirrels, rabbits and prairie dogs. Blaze was the only boy allowed to join the tribesmen on the further expeditions, some overnight, in search of larger game.

Just before the cotton harvest, Blaze had shot a full grown deer and further enhanced his reputation as a hunter. Even his father, who had discouraged his interest in hunting, seemed proud of him.

"So, what's the wager for the big contest?" Setting Sun asked.

"You need a wager for a contest like this?" Blaze asked, exaggerating disgust in his voice.

"Of course," Setting Sun replied proudly.

"We shall discuss it after you get your arrowhead. Before that, though, let me get you more poultice for that nasty cut on your arm. Maybe I'll wager a pot of the cactus poultice I soaked yesterday. From the looks of it, you could use that more than silly beads or even arrowheads. When was the last time you hunted? Why do you even want arrowheads?"

"Because they mean a lot to you," Setting Sun said, and smiled. "And why should I wager for poultice? As a giver of medicine, you must treat me as necessary."

He was right, Blaze thought. Any man or woman blessed with the gift of medicine must treat all that are in need, even visitors to the Great Cliff. Sinagua men and women did not trade for medicine, as they did for clothing or food or pottery. If Blaze agreed to learn the art of medicine, he would be expected to treat all in the tribe, and every family of the Great Cliff would contribute what was necessary for him to live and work. Blaze had always enjoyed helping Desert Cloud, especially when it meant that he could spend more time hunting and gathering and less time in the fields. He had even thought for a while that he might like to learn the art of medicine. He had certainly practiced that skill as much as ever, treating the scrapes and wounds of the guayball competitors. But since he had begun playing guayball, he had thought of medicine less, even as he found himself using those skills more.

The boys made their way back to the cliff through the cool fall air. Usually, Blaze hated winter, because prey was scarcer and there was less to do. But as much as Blaze disliked farm work, doing nothing was worse.

While the women and girls tended the young children and prepared food through the winter, the men and boys spent much of the cold season idly playing games of chance. It was Setting Sun's favorite time of the year. Only the weavers, like Great Bear and Tall Grass, worked throughout the winter moons without stop. The men with other skills, like Strong Hands, who made jewelry, and Coyote Claw, who was a stone cutter, had some work to do, yet still had plenty of idle time as well.

For Blaze, this winter would be the best ever. With no work in the fields, he would have time every day for guayball. He had not told anyone yet, but his dream was to train a pod to be strong enough to travel to Hohokam land and compete against Stonah's pod. A victory against Bravegart's West Village pod would be even sweeter.

Of course it was only a foolish idea, but Blaze liked to imagine his pod from the Great Cliff traveling from one Hohokam village to another, challenging local guayball pods. If they were good enough, they could wager valuable goods, and bring back enormous wealth to their village.

Blaze knew that the elders would never approve of such a childish scheme. The elders barely allowed their informal guayball games. Blaze's grandfather had argued before the grand elders that it was a harmless pastime, and might even improve the hunting skills of the young competitors. The grand elders had approved the playing of the game, but only for a short time, so they could see whether guayball would or would not divert interest from the task of farming. There were elders who were worried about a Hohokam attack, and believed that guayball might prepare the young to better defend the tribe. But as time went on and the threat of attack lessened, those elders might once more discourage the playing of any game by the young men and older boys of the Great Cliff. And they would never allow anyone to leave the village in order to compete.

Still, Blaze loved to think about his traveling guayball pod. He knew it was a silly dream. Or was it?

CHAPTER 17

▼

"Another guayball injury?" Swift Deer asked as he stepped through the small door and into their home.

"Just some sand in my eye," Blaze said, lying back on the hard corn husk mat on the floor, and pressing a wad of mesquite sap to his left eye.

"At least that foolish game is giving you more practice at the healing arts," Blaze's father said, shaking his head. "Desert Cloud told me that you have been a most promising student of medicine ever since you returned from your journey and began playing that grayball game."

"Guayball," Blaze said.

"What?"

"Guayball, Father. The game is called guayball."

"Whatever it is named, it is a foolish waste of time."

"But Father, it is an important religious rite in the Hohokam tribe. They are celebrating the original battles of their gods in the Underworld before their God of the Sun won command."

"*Our* gods never battled. Father Sun has always reigned among the gods of the Sinaguas."

"Swift Deer," Blaze's mother said while rolling ground corn and water into balls, "Grandfather does say that the Hohokam people are a great hunting tribe, and with our people less blessed with rain, hunting is becoming more important to feed our people."

"If we spent less time hunting and playing war games," said Swift Deer, "and tried to be less like Hohokam and more like Sinaguas, then the God of the Rain might look more kindly upon us and bless us as he has done in the past!"

What if his father was right about that? His father was right about him wanting to be more like a Hohokam than a Sinagua. He did love hunting and guayball more than working the fields.

"The grand elders are deciding whether to allow the young Sinaguas to continue to play that Hohokam game," Swift Deer stated.

Blaze looked up, stunned. They might forbid guayball? They couldn't do that!

"But Father," Blaze protested. "Why?"

"Blaze, you are young and foolish. Do you not see what this game has done to the Hohokam people? They used to be a peaceful tribe. Now, you can see what they have become. You know better than anyone. When you train young men in the art of war, they will want to fight. Our journeyers to Hohokam almost did not return. That would have triggered a terrible war. Many elders still fear that the Hohokam people might yet attack us. That is why we have doubled our guards."

It was no use arguing with his father. For one thing, Swift Deer did not make the rules. For another thing, respect for elders was absolute among Sinagua people. His father just did not understand. There were many good Hohokam people who played guayball. People like Stonah.

"Father," Bay Leaf said as she dropped the rolled corn balls into the pot of boiling water hanging over fire, "I like watching the boys play. They just want to have fun."

"Great Father, forgive my dear daughter," Swift Deer said, bowing towards the ground. "Many are not boys any more. I am told that Running Stream, Strong Horn, Large Rock and Fleet Foot play that game. They have all come of age and are adult Sinagua tribesmen. Their animal spirits all came to them before they were introduced to that ball game. Your animal spirit has yet to come to you, Blaze. I think it is waiting until you put aside the games of childhood, such as your ball game."

"My daughter," Lightfoot said to Bay Leaf, "perhaps you spend too much time looking at those young men play their boy games. Maybe you should be spending more time with your painted woman. Your womanhood ritual will be here before the winter's snow has moved on. There is still much that you must learn from her."

"Maybe she should watch us play guayball more often," Blaze said teasingly. "She will better be able to choose a mate after her ritual. But maybe that is not necessary. I see the way she looks at Running Stream."

Bay Leaf tried to hide the blush of her cheeks. Lightfoot smiled ever so slightly.

"There are still many moons until her womanhood ritual," Swift Deer said. "The Great Rain Dance is tomorrow night. All the girls-soon-to-be-women participate. I hope that she is ready for this."

Swift Deer spoke only to his wife, and looked to her as if the responsibility for their daughter were hers alone.

Bay Leaf had always been part of Blaze's life. It saddened him that by next harvest, she would be a woman, and probably a wife to a man of the tribe. She might soon have her own family.

Bay Leaf was a good sister and had always played with him as an equal. She had a good spirit, and while they had often teased each other, Blaze knew that Bay Leaf was fond of him and had respect for him as well. While Blaze had great affection for his sister, it did bother him that all she needed to do was turn fifteen harvests of age and learn a few rituals, and she became a Sinagua woman. It was not fair. Blaze was required to make a large game kill and have his animal spirit come to him before he could have his manhood ritual.

Blaze was fairly confident that his animal spirit, the spirit of the mountain lion, would come to him when it left its earthly body. But when would that be? And what if his father was right? What if his animal spirit was waiting for him to give up games of children, in particular the game of guayball?

CHAPTER 18

▼

"Grandfather," Blaze said, "should I not compete in this game of guay-ball tomorrow?"

In his usual corner of the Great Room, the white-haired man was adding small amounts of crushed soapstone to his large bowl of clay and mixing them with a strong stick.

"That is a decision that only you can make," the old man spoke in a soft voice as he looked up from his work while his hands continued to stir. Blaze's grandfather would know when the clay was ready by the feel of it.

"My father believes that I should not," Blaze said.

"Has he forbidden it?"

"You know he would not. That is a decision that only the grand elders can make."

Lion Heart stopped stirring and reached his hands into the bowl, pushing the clay through his fingers much like Blaze's mother kneaded corn dough.

"Then it is your decision," he said.

"But Grandfather, what if my father is right, and the rain has stopped coming because we have insulted the gods by playing guay-ball?"

"That certainly is possible."

"Then I should stop playing?" Blaze asked in a teary voice.

"I did not say that," Lion Heart spoke, as he reached for a large, coiled stick frame. "While what you say is possible, there may be other causes for the drought, and the skills of the warrior could be of greater importance in the years ahead."

"Do you mean if we get into a war with the Hohokam?"

"The Hohokam, or the Anasazi, or the Mogollons. I have said many times that when food grows scarce, conflicts arise. You have seen that yourself with the Hohokam. I have watched you compete in this game of guayball. It molds the body and heart of a warrior. A warrior must be brave, strong, and quick, and must ignore pain. A great warrior must be a leader, able to plan carefully before a battle and make immediate decisions in the midst of a fight."

"But Grandfather, what about the skills of a warrior, such as the use of a knife or a spear or an arrow? What about the hand-to-hand fighting that you have taught me?"

"Blaze," Lion Heart explained while using his hands to apply a coat of the tempered clay to the coiled frame, "those skills can be taught quickly, and most are little different than the hunting skills that all young boys already learn. But training the heart and soul of a warrior is a more difficult task, and takes much more time. I see this game of guayball doing that. And in you, I have seen the traits of a fine warrior and great leader of men."

A swell of pride filled Blaze's chest as his eyes followed the skilled hands of his grandfather at work. Lion Heart was the only man in the Great Cliff who made pottery. Blaze was told that his grandmother had been the most skilled potter in the village. Their dwelling still was filled with many of her beautiful and useful containers. When she died, Blaze's grandfather took up making pots, carrying on the tradition of his wife. Lion Heart never decorated them as his wife had, but he was known for making fine pots that last.

Blaze was struck by the size of the pot his grandfather was shaping. Lion Heart usually molded small pots around gourds of winter squash.

That way, when the clay dried and hardened, he could wait until the squash rotted, and dig it out, leaving a clean, hollow pot. But this pot was larger than any his grandfather had made before.

"Why are you making it so big?"

"The grand elders have decided to increase our food and water storage, and this pot will hold much water. As you know, in the stock rooms and pits on each floor of the cliff, we keep enough food and water for two moons. With the threat of attack, it has been decided that we need to increase our reserves. These large pots will hold extra water should we find ourselves defending our Great Cliff."

War! The grand elders were really worried about war! A shudder of fear tinged with excitement ran up Blaze's spine.

"Grandfather, tell me again about the war you were in."

"Ah, war," the old man said, laying down his large, partially coated piece of pottery. He looked straight into the eyes of his grandchild and continued. "I hear the eagerness in your voice. Many great warriors do hope to fight. Some even create excuses for war. Yet the truly great leader will seek peaceful resolution to conflict, but not be afraid to fight when necessary.

"And yes, Blaze, I was in a war. I was a young child, not much older than you are now. It was the Mogollons who attacked us. We had a drought back then, almost as severe as the one we have now, and our well kept us better supplied with water than the Mogollons were. They lived in a land south of us, where the sun is even hotter. We had what they wanted, water. They drove us from the well and we retreated to the cliff, where we were safe. But after many years of peace, we had not expected war. We did not have the food and water stored in the cliff to last us enough moons to outwait our attackers. We had more than one hundred people living in the Great Cliff.

"The Mogollons had us trapped in our cliff dwellings. When our food and water ran low enough, we were forced to attack. We sent every person who could fight, even old men and young boys. Had we lost, it would have been the end of our Sinagua people. We surprised them at night and fought with the heart of a trapped mother bear. We were not afraid to die in battle because death was certain if we did not fight. We lost many men and boys, almost half the men of our tribe. Our women did much of the men's work for years afterwards. There were more Mogollons than Sinaguas that day, and they could have defeated us then, but they had already paid a steep price in lives, and they were not willing to pay the higher price necessary for complete victory.

"They had the choice of returning home with more of their warriors alive, and so they stopped fighting. They had expected that against their great numbers, we would fall more easily. We did not."

Lion Heart picked up the large coiled frame and continued to grab handfuls of clay. He applied it with his dark weathered hands, gently smoothing it with his rough fingers.

"But war is a terrible thing," he continued as he reached for more clay. "I saw my father slain right before me. An arrow went clear through his neck. He was so brave, he pulled it out himself. The pain must have been overwhelming, but he did not want to frighten me, and he did not cry out. He tried to speak to me, but the hole in his throat made it impossible for him to form words. He so badly wanted to communicate, and when I cried to him that I could not understand, I saw great tears stream down his face. He died as I was wiping away the tears. I was ashamed that this great warrior was crying, and I did not want others to see that. I pray that my father did not know the coldness in my heart.

"Not a day goes by when I don't recall that terrible moment, and regret my hard heart. I lost two brothers in that battle, but we were victorious. I was so excited about fighting myself and winning, that it took a long time until the pain of losing so much of my family hit me. War is a terrible thing, Blaze. Sometimes necessary, but always terrible."

Blaze swallowed. His grandfather was a wise man, and Blaze did believe that war was something to be avoided. But if war happened, he wanted to be ready. The urge to fight continued to grow within him. Meanwhile, he would continue to play guayball. His grandfather had given him permission to play. He had even encouraged it. But the need to compete was so great in his heart that Blaze knew he would have played anyway. Nothing could stop him from playing this game he had grown to love so much. He could not wait for his big guayball contest against the Lower Cliff pod.

CHAPTER 19

▼

As the last light of Father Sun faded overhead, the quiet chanting of the medicine woman echoed throughout the large room. As she sang, Desert Cloud carefully applied the final color to her sand painting on the floor. The flickering fire in the center of the Great Room gave an orange hue to the sandstone dust depicting the falling rain. Above charcoal colored clouds, the medicine woman sprinkled dried corn dust for the yellow sun that would shine upon the wet fields after the rains.

The children of the Great Cliff knelt shoulder to shoulder, surrounding the holy woman at her work. Towering above the other children, Blaze prayed that the following year he would be a man of the tribe. Then, he would no longer be waiting for the arrival of the Rain Spirits. Instead, he would be one of them. Still, the small child within him eagerly awaited their entry.

The Sinaguas were a people of few ceremonies. From travelers, Blaze knew of the many tribes where nearly every action of daily life was a ritual or a celebration. Stonah had spoken of the many elaborate and sacred rites the Hohokam held in their Great Plaza. Their blood sacrifices had most intrigued Blaze. The Sinaguas of the Great Cliff gathered in ceremony only for death, rain, mating and coming of age.

Death was a small, quiet ritual, while the Dance of Rain was their greatest ceremony.

Blaze's earliest memories in life were of the Dance of Rain. He loved the chants, the drums, the sand art, and the dance of the marked men. Just having all the people of the cliff crowded into the Great Room created an excitement unlike any other. So many people gathered in one place had always brought about a sense of awe in Blaze, but after visiting the great village of the Hokokam, the fifty-three Sinaguas of his village seemed no more than a drop in a giant water pot.

Crouched next to Blaze was Setting Sun. His eyes were aglow with the flickering reflection of the fire's light. He seemed as excited as Blaze as they awaited the arrival of the Rain Spirits.

The soft boom of the drums rang out from the bottom of the cliff. The chant of the Rain Spirits intermingled magically with the beat of the drum. Blaze shivered with excitement and awe. The chanting grew louder as the voices rose to the top of their cliff dwelling. They must be on the second level by now, Blaze thought. As their rhythmic chant rose to the third and then the fourth level of their cliff home, the excitement reached a climactic pitch. Blaze turned around and saw a mix of fear and joy on his baby sister's face. While this was her second Dance of Rain, she would have been too young to remember her first. Chittanberry sat upright next to Blaze with their mother crouched behind, holding a hand firmly on the baby's shoulder.

And then the first of the beautiful and mysterious masked figures appeared on the ledge outside the doorway. More followed, until there was no more room on the ledge. The first Rain Spirit to enter the Great Room wore a bright yellow mask with red circles painted on each cheek and black circles surrounding the eyes. Some masks were funny while others were scary. Some portrayed animals; others resembled the gods.

Blaze knew that the Rain Spirits were really the younger tribesmen behind those masks. Many generations ago, the actual Rain Spirits had visited the people of Sinagua. Those godlings, half human and half spirit, had danced and danced, and caused the rain to fall in abundance. Those spirit-humans also taught the Sinagua people many of their most important skills, in the areas of farming, hunting, weaving and medicine. The real Rain Spirits no longer visited, but each harvest, tribesmen would portray those spirit-human visitors of the past, and dance and sing the sacred chants which would bring rain to their land during the next growing season.

It was said that the drums and the chants drew the real Rain Spirits into the souls of the masked men. That was why it was so important that the village men learn the chants precisely, otherwise the true Rain Spirits would fail to possess them for the Dance of Rain.

One of the eight dancing Rain Spirits approached and handed each child a quid from the agave plant. Blaze greedily grabbed his piece and popped it right into his mouth. The first bite was always the best. He sunk his teeth into the quid, and the sweet juices burst over his tongue. The juice mixed with his saliva for the best taste in the world. Blaze chewed some more and finally swallowed the sweet liquid. Delicious! He continued to sink his teeth into the quid and each chew brought more flavor, but none of the bites quite equaled that first one.

The children held out their hands for more quids, even though the ones in their mouths could last forever. They wanted more of that sweetness from the first bite. Blaze saw Setting Sun putting quids into his side pouch. Setting Sun always saved some for wagering in the coming weeks. Unchewed quids from the Dance of Rain were always in high demand.

Blaze dropped a second quid on his tongue. Yum! He remembered how he used to fill his mouth with so many quids that he could barely breath. He saw some of the younger children doing the same, and smiled.

As the Rain Spirits continued to chant and dance, the women opened the food pots and passed out cornbread covered with a sweet hackberry sauce and crushed black walnuts. Blaze got up along with many other children and spit his quid into the fire so that he could eat the sweetened cornbread.

After the children and adults had their fill of the sweet bread, the drums stopped and the Rain Spirits gathered around the fire. Desert Cloud chanted her special Song of Rain, and then Great Bear, the Chief Elder, spoke.

"For a number of harvests we have performed this Dance of Rain, but the rain has not been plentiful. We will continue to ask for the help of the Rain Spirits, but I fear more is asked of us by the gods below.

"The grand elders have discussed this at length, and we have decided that everyone must do their part. The young tribesmen will learn a new chant for a second Dance of Rain that we will enact during the moon of the planting. It will be in addition to our traditional Dance of the Rain that we celebrate each harvest."

Great Bear paused. A second Dance of Rain! Blaze thought that was a great idea. The God of Rain would surely be pleased. Also, a Dance of Rain celebration was always fun.

"All Sinagua men, women and children will begin to dig a new irrigation ditch from the well, diverting what remains there to our settlement."

That sounded like a lot of extra work, and would take away from valuable hunting time, but they did need the water, and Blaze thought the plan was good.

"Finally, we must not offend Father Corn. All of our energy must go into the growing of food. I fear that too much of our young people's energy is directed to the art of war, and is angering Father Corn. And so all warlike games, which includes this game they call guayball, are forbidden to the boys and young men of the cliff."

No guayball? That could not be! Blaze *lived* for that game! The deciding game between the Upper Cliff pod and the Lower Cliff pod was to be played the next day! Blaze had thought of little else in the past day.

Blaze and Setting Sun looked at each other in disbelief. Blaze turned around and saw his grandfather just staring ahead stone faced.

Great Bear's a coward, and he's foolish, Blaze thought angrily. The grand elder had always been afraid of fighting. He will be the cause of ruin for these Sinagua people. And if we do survive, he will lead a tribe that Blaze did not want to be part of.

Blaze tried to image days of more farm work and less hunting. And he thought about long winter days without guayball. He felt sick inside. Sick and enraged.

No, he could not stay with these people. Blaze decided then and there that he would go to a place where he could follow his true destiny as a hunter and a warrior. A place where he would not only play guayball, but be highly respected for his skill in that game.

CHAPTER 20

▼

As the last of the fiery orange ball sank below the rocky landscape of the canyon, Blaze thanked Father Sun for another good trip across the sky. Away for a full day, he knew that his people would be starting to miss him by now.

It pained him not to tell anyone of his plans to leave, but he feared that had he told Setting Sun, his friend might have told the elders, and they would have sent out a party of tribesmen to bring him back. Blaze had not told his grandfather either. If anyone would understand what he had done, it would be his grandfather. But what if Lion Heart had objected? His grandfather surely would have been able to talk him out of leaving. Blaze had also avoided speaking to Desert Cloud. After the great honor that the medicine woman had bestowed upon him, he had been too ashamed to face her one last time.

Leaving without saying goodbye to his mother had been the hardest part of the past day. He saw how protective she was with Chittanberry, always keeping the little girl so close. While Blaze was no longer strapped to a cradleboard, he knew his mother still worried about him, and needed to keep him nearby, too. Before his journey, Lightfoot had not spoken a word about her fears, but he knew that she had worried about him for many moons before he had left. He still could picture the relief in her eyes on the day he returned home. Had he told his mother, she would have begged him to stay, and he would not have had the heart to do otherwise.

If his father was upset, that was okay with Blaze. Swift Deer was an important elder in the village, and Blaze was certain that his father had helped persuade Great Bear to forbid guayball. Still, it had been easier to leave without confronting his father.

And so Blaze had slipped away from the cliff at first sun and started off to Hohokam land. He knew that he would make a great Hohokam brave. He was sure that his arrow would earn him respect as a hunter, and his speed and skill would win him praise as a guayball player. He only hoped that they would accept him into their tribe with his flat head.

During that first day of traveling, Blaze had made his way through the rocky territory as quickly as possible. Trying to recall the route from his journey had taken great effort, but he kept the rising sun to his left and the setting sun to his right, and did his best to remember the paths he had traveled. Blaze was confident that he had stayed on the right trail so far. Yet as the sun dropped low in the pink sky, the elk-shaped shadow of the canyon ahead was not familiar.

As a coyote howled in the distance, Blaze reached into his carry pouch for a piece of dried deer meat. Only when the food touched his tongue did he realize how hungry he was.

It was a cool evening, and Blaze shivered, but not from the chill in the air. He was alone in the dark, and not sure exactly where he was. And deep down, he was not sure that he was doing the right thing. He continued to eat until the only light in the sky was cast by the stars.

A coyote was howling again when Blaze heard something else, something closer by. It sounded almost like a snarl. His heart nearly stopped. A mountain lion! What if it were a mountain lion? Blaze put down his meat and grabbed his bow, nervously slipping in an arrow. He turned his head slowly in each direction, straining his ears to detect the slightest sound. Shadows from balls of snakeweed dotted the dark, flat land surrounding him. Wait, he said to himself. What if those shadows were not snakeweed shrubs? What if one was a mountain lion? Then a terrible thought struck him.

Since he had abandoned his tribe, would his animal spirit still become part of him? Or was the thing out there, making that sound, the spirit of the mountain lion coming to him now? Would his animal spirit be angry with him for leaving his people? Was the mountain lion coming to punish him? To kill him?

Fear crept over Blaze. It gnawed at his heart and spread slowly from there until panic gripped each bone and muscle in his body.

Standing alone in the desert night after a hard day of travel, Blaze's legs had begun to tire. On his journey, it had taken his party five long days to make their trip to Hohokam land, but that had been carrying goods to trade. Moving along with only a bow and arrow, a small food pouch, and a water bag, Blaze was sure that he had covered much more distance. At his current pace, he would surely complete his journey in three days.

Still holding his arrow ready to shoot, Blaze waited, but nothing happened. After more time went by, his panic began to lessen and weariness set in. Finally, he sat down. He leaned back against a large boulder, so that he only had to look forward and to his sides to protect himself. Even a mountain lion could not climb the cliff above him. Or could it?

Sitting there, fear once again grew within him, along with fatigue. Afraid the slightest noise would alert an attacking mountain lion, or whatever was lurking out there, Blaze did not dare move a muscle. Instead, he focused all his energy on all the sounds of the night. He thought he heard a soft crinkling noise to his side. His eyes searched the shadows of the few trees dotting the dry plain. Did he hear the wind rustling dry leaves, or was it an animal stepping through the sparse undergrowth?

The night had never scared Blaze as it had other boys and girls. He was a hunter. Yet this night was different. Exhausted, his eyelids became heavy. Still worried, his mind worked to stay alert. As he remained motionless, fear and fatigue battled within him.

The next thing he knew, he was opening his eyes. It was morning! He must have fallen asleep! Blaze tried to move, but struggled to overcome the stiffness that had set in from sitting against hard rock for so long. In spite of his neck and back pain, the first rays of warmth from Father Sun felt good on his face.

Blaze searched for the piece of meat that he had been eating. It was gone! A wave of fear gripped him. Where had it gone? Who had taken it? Was it the mountain lion? Or merely a scavenging bird or animal? He had survived the night, though, and his hunger and thirst began to rise above his fear.

Blaze reached for his food pouch to get more dried meat, but the pouch was no longer next to him. Fear clutched him once more. Still holding his bow, he quickly drew back an arrow. His eyes were searching the dry valley floor ahead, when off in the distance he spotted a brown piece of leather. Was it his food bag? Blaze stood and stepped carefully toward it. It *was* his bag! He ran and grabbed the leather pouch, but it was empty.

Where was his food? Blaze looked again at his empty food pouch. There was no sign of an animal clawing it open, but he couldn't be sure. He plodded back to the boulder where he had slept, and reached for his water bag. He prayed that whoever or whatever had taken his food had left him his water. His round water bag was resting where he had put it down and was still half full. Thank you, Father Sun! Blaze grabbed the bag and greedily began to pour water into his dry mouth and down his parched throat.

"Stop!" he told himself. He knew that he had to conserve his water. While there were a number of watering holes between Sinagua and Hohokam, he did not trust his memory to find them all. He knew that thirst would be his most dangerous enemy. A desert rat can draw liquid from seeds and never has to drink, and the desert tortoise can quench its thirst with the moisture in grasses and flowers, but a human needs to drink real water to survive.

Blaze had made the right decision when he chose to bring the larger bag. It was lined with the bladder of a mule deer and covered with leather from that deer's hide. Blaze tied the top of the water bag shut, and strapped it to his breechcloth. He attached the empty food bag as well, and set off in the direction of Hohokam land. He knew he must find food, and soon, but that did not worry him. Small game always abounded, and Blaze trusted his skill with the arrow.

With Father Sun rising to his left, Blaze forged ahead. He shut from his mind the life he was leaving behind, and focused on the desert journey before him. He tried to think about his future tribe, a tribe with more guayball arenas than there were men in his own tiny village at the cliff. Yet marching alone across the desert, guayball was starting to lose its allure. He didn't know why. He hoped he would feel differently when he got to Snaketown and played again. He tried to recall that incredible feeling of competing, of running his hardest, hitting a rival player and making a perfect lead pass. Blaze tried to reignite that spark in his soul, that spark from guayball that made him feel so alive. But the fire was gone. Still, he had made his decision, and so he pressed on towards his new home.

CHAPTER 21

▼

Blaze chewed and chewed, but his mouth remained bone dry. The hard quid brought no relief to his thirst. He finally spit his quid to the ground.

The rocky hills ahead looked vaguely familiar, but then, most rocky hills look alike when you do not know them. It was his third day of traveling and high sun was nearly upon him. Blaze knew that he should find a shaded spot to rest. Even in the cooler harvest season, the mid-day sun was intense. It was Father Sun's great gift and great curse.

But Blaze would not stop. He needed to get to Hohokam land soon. Badly in need of water, he could not go on much longer. He felt that he had a better chance of finding water or a village in the light of day. After dark, he might miss the signs of a distant watering hole, or he might fail to recognize a landmark that could guide him to his new home.

Blaze had filled his water bag just once, early on his second day, but he had run most of that day. Not stopping for high sun, he had limited himself to one sip at a time. By dark, his water had been gone.

At least the second night had been better than the first. If the silence of the desert night had been broken again by the howls of its nocturnal creatures, Blaze did not know it. Exhausted, he had eaten a handful of wild berries and the crown of an agave plant. Immediately afterwards, he had fallen asleep.

Blaze searched the horizon for a sign of water. His eyes were drawn to what looked like a small prickly pear cactus in the distance. Yet the desert can play tricks on the eyes, especially in the midday heat. He cautiously approached, trying hard not to get his hopes too high. As he got nearer, he was sure that what he saw really was his prickly desert friend! Blaze ran the last few lengths to the hard green succulent.

There was moisture in this desert plant. The ratlike javelina, with its mouth as tough as leather, would chomp through the cactus, spines and all, eating the whole thing. A human could not do that. Instead, Blaze grabbed his knife, and carefully removed the thorns, throwing them on the ground. At home, those thorns would make valuable needles for the making of cloth and the stitching of wounds, and he would never waste them, but alone in the desert, he could think only of his immediate survival. He carved a layer from the fruit of the plant and put it in his mouth. Nothing had ever tasted so good! The slightly sweet wetness of the cactus spread over his tongue and slid down his parched throat. He continued to peel away layers and suck them as the terrible dryness in his mouth subsided. He was still thirsty, but his mouth no longer felt like hot, dry sand.

And then Blaze spotted familiar holes in the ground ahead. Of course! Cactus meant water and water meant animal life. Below him was a town of prairie dogs! He knew those holes anywhere!

Suddenly, at the thought of fresh meat, his hands shook with hunger. He breathed slowly to settle himself. He knew how to hunt prairie dogs. High sun was a harder time to blind the animals, but late in the harvest season, the sun was lower than in mid-summer, and he was sure that he could do it.

First, he needed to find something to reflect the sun. At home, a piece of mica or pitch-glazed stone was used. Setting Sun always had something that would work in his bag of beads. Blaze wondered what he could use here. Around his neck hung the shiny golden sun his father had given him. Swift Deer had said that as long as he wore it, Father Sun would look with favor upon him.

Light or no light, Blaze knew that he could easily shoot the first animal to leave the hole. One prairie dog, though, would not provide him enough meat. He would need more. But by the time he loaded a second arrow onto his bow, any other prairie dogs would be back to the safety of their home under the ground. Instead, if he set up his golden necklace to reflect the bright sun into the entrance of the hole, the animals would be momentarily blinded when they emerged, and he would be able to easily shoot many of them. Yes, he needed to use the necklace.

"Wear it always, my son," Blaze's father had said to him. Could this be how Father Sun would help him? Maybe he was meant to take it off and use it to survive.

"Father Sun, I pray for your permission to remove this necklace so that you may assist me in my time of need."

With those words, Blaze bowed towards the sun above, and removed his necklace. He quietly approached the entrance to the hole, and angled his shiny golden medallion so that it reflected the sun's strong rays into the ground. Blaze then backed off and found a cool spot under a natural stone ledge where he would wait.

It was good to escape the midday heat. After so much traveling and so little eating and drinking, exhaustion was beginning to overtake him. He fought sleep, knowing that if he did not get the prairie dogs as they emerged from the hole, then he might not get them at all. And he needed to eat.

After a long time, a burrowing sound arose from the hole. Moments later, a flat brown nose poked out of the ground. It turned its head in all directions, sniffing the surrounding dirt, and then its whole head emerged. Its dark eyes peered around as the furry animal turned its neck in a nearly complete circle. It climbed out of its hole and waddled unsteadily ahead. Blaze could tell by the way the prairie dog moved that it had been blinded by the reflected sunlight. Another prairie dog followed, and then another, and another after that.

Blaze drew back his arrow and fired. The arrow struck the fat mid-section of the first animal. Blaze loaded another arrow onto his bow, and aimed at a second animal and shot. Another hit! Should he try for one more? If he could not find his way soon to Hohokam land, he might need the meat, but he did not want to kill this creature if it was not necessary. Also, skinning the animal would take time, and he wanted to move on as quickly as possible.

But the thought of being lost in the desert without food scared him. Blaze knew the importance of meat on a journey, and so he loaded a third arrow, and drew it back. Two prairie dogs were bumping into each other as they furiously struggled in their blindness to find the passageway to their underground village. Blaze fired and another ball of fur collapsed on the ground. That would suffice, he thought.

He used his knife to cut away the hide from the first animal he had shot. He sliced the choice meat, and did the same with the next two prairie dogs. Then Blaze looked around for tinder and a hearth to start a fire.

He spotted a dead yucca shrub nearby and went over to it. He stripped the tall, stout stem of its needles, and used his knife to shave down its few bumps and sharp spots. The top of the stem would make a good drill. The base was dried and almost split, and would make a good hearth. Blaze snapped off the bottom. Finally, he arose and scoured the area for good tinder. He grabbed a dead branch of sagebrush, and shredded the bark with his knife. From his side pouch, he grabbed a handful of cattail down, and pulled it apart until it was fluffy. After mixing the whitish-gray down with his bark, he placed it next to the yucca. He decided that it was a good tinder and would ignite well. Next, he took his knife and carved a drill from the smooth yucca branch, and notched the side of the yucca stalk, which would serve as his hearth.

With steady downward pressure onto the flat hearth, Blaze twirled the drill between his palms, creating friction between the two pieces of wood. He continued to drill until he felt heat, and a pile of charred powder began to form. As the powder gathered and grew hotter, Blaze transferred it to his collection of tinder, and blew. No flame. Please light, he thought! Blaze drilled some more, trying again to ignite the tinder. Suddenly a spark caught the ball of down and shaved bark, and a flame burst within it. Blaze fed the flame some of the fine wood shavings and then larger yucca branches, and soon he was looking at a roaring fire.

Using his knife to hold a large piece of meat over the fire, Blaze charred both sides and took his first bite. It was delicious! In no time, Blaze had eaten all the meat from the first of his fallen prey.

Blaze cooked the skinned meat from the next two prairie dogs, and tied it to his breechcloth. The sun would dry it as he traveled. Dried meat would last longer and might be the difference between life and death in the desert.

CHAPTER 22

▼

Chewing the hard meat, Blaze tried to draw any liquid he could from it. It had tasted better the day before, immediately after killing and cooking it. Now, he needed to find water. The small amount of juice he had drawn from the cactus was not enough to keep him going. It had quenched his thirst for the night, but a new sun had brought an even greater need for water. He could think of nothing but water. He needed water to live. He had always trusted his hunting and scavenging skills, but for the first time in his life, he worried about dying in the desert.

Death had never scared Blaze very much. He knew that he would join the spirits of his ancestors in the Great Underground. But now that he had abandoned his people, would those same ancestors still welcome him? He was no longer a Sinagua, and not yet a Hohokam. Blaze worried that if he died on this journey, he would be truly alone in the next life. And so, for the first time, death did frighten him.

The further Blaze traveled from the Great Cliff, the more he feared he had made a mistake in leaving. He was aware of the hurt that he certainly caused his sisters and mother. Even Setting Sun had to be crushed. That's the way Blaze would feel if Setting Sun had left instead. Blaze's father, too, must be hurt and shamed. And even though Blaze was angry at all the village elders who had forced him to leave, he still did not wish to cause his father pain.

Blaze could not put aside thoughts of his family, even of his brothers whose bones lay in the wall of their dwelling. He recalled what his mother had said about his father and New Moon. He couldn't get his mother's words out of his mind, yet he still could not imagine Swift Deer so affectionate with an infant. His father had never been very loving with either him or his sisters, but maybe there was a reason for that.

Nevertheless, returning to his people and to cliff life was something that Blaze could not do. He wished that he had been born a Hohokam. Then it would be easy. He could be a great hunter and a competitor in the ball arenas, and be respected for the skills he most valued.

Could the Hohokam ever truly be his people? Travelers did sometimes join new tribes. Even some of the Sinaguas of the Great Cliff had come from other peoples. What did the Spirit of the Corn and Father Sun expect Blaze to do? Why would they give him the spirit of a warrior if he could not use it for his people? Why would his animal spirit be that of the mountain lion if he were destined to spend his days farming the land?

Blaze tried to push these thoughts out of his mind, and focus on the task before him. He needed water. With the sun starting it's journey down from its midday height, Blaze kept the fiery yellow god to his right, moving towards where he thought Hohokam land should be. He again scanned the dry land in front of him, hoping to spot a familiar landmark. The outline of a low cliff started to look like something he had seen before.

Trudging forward one step at a time, Blaze heard the shuffling of feet to his left. As he turned, a voice boomed, "Stop!"

Instantly Blaze grabbed for his bow. A boy stepped out from behind a rock and yelled, "No!"

The boy's drawn arrow was aimed right at Blaze's chest. Blaze dropped his own bow and stared at the armed boy before him. He was short with pale skin and long wavy brown hair hanging loosely around his face. Blaze knew this boy! He had played guayball with him! Actually, he had played against him. This was one of the boys from the West pod, one of Blaze's opponents!

"Cliff boy, what brings you here?"

Blaze was speechless. He could not tell the boy why he had come, not while he was being held captive.

"Speak!" the boy commanded.

"I have come to find Stonah."

The Hohokam boy nodded.

"Walk that way," he said, pointing towards the open land ahead.

"Will you take me to Stonah?"

"No," the boy said.

"Why not?" Blaze asked.

"I cannot say. You must come with me."

Blaze nodded. What else could he do? Where was this boy taking him? To Bravegart? Blaze shuddered.

"Could I have water?" Blaze asked.

The boy released the tension in his bow. Then, holding his weapon with one hand, the boy pulled a water bag from his waist strap with his other hand. He tossed it to Blaze, who caught it and without hesitation drank. It was incredible how good the warm liquid felt as it hit his mouth and ran down his throat. Blaze drank about half the bottle and stopped. He wanted the rest but it would be impolite to drink more.

Blaze calculated the distance between himself and the Hohokam boy. Was he close enough to attack before the boy could draw back his arrow and fire? Blaze was not sure. Better to play it safe, he thought, and so he tied the top of the water bag shut and tossed it back.

They walked further, not exchanging any words at all. As the land around them grew greener, Blaze knew that they must be near the corn and bean fields surrounding Snaketown. Finally, the boy called out a strange word, and another Hohokam child appeared. This was a boy Blaze did not recognize. He was a little younger than Blaze.

"Derskin, stay here with this cliff boy. Be careful with him. He may be dangerous. I need to go into the village. I will return shortly."

Then the older boy stepped forward and grabbed Blaze's weapons from the ground, and handed them to the new boy, Derskin.

"Gratewat, who is he?"

"He is Blaze, of the Great Cliff."

"A flathead!"

"A Sinaguan," Gratewat said.

The younger boy put an arrow in Blaze's bow, and then smiled mischievously.

"Say nothing to him. Shoot him only if he runs," Gratewat commanded, and ran off.

Blaze warily eyed the young Hohokam boy. Without a bow or a knife, Blaze wondered how he could escape?

"I need more water," Blaze said.

Derskin said nothing.

"My bag is empty," Blaze said. "I have been in the desert for four days. Please, where can I fill my water bag?"

The young Hohokam boy nodded towards his right, indicating that Blaze move there. He walked while Derskin trailed him with drawn bow. They rounded a dirt hill spotted with short dry green shrubs. To the side of the hill was one of the Hohokam canals. It was smaller than the ones Blaze had seen on his first journey, with only a trickle of liquid moving through it.

He turned around to face Derskin, and asked, "May I fill my bag?"

The boy nodded. Blaze filled the leather bag to the top with water and ravenously drank the entire bagful. He filled it again, then reached to his waist and loosened a piece of meat hanging from his breechcloth. He put the dried meat into his mouth, and with a moist tongue, the juices of the meat flowed freely. It tasted delicious!

Blaze noticed the boy eyeing the food in his hand. An idea came to him at once.

"Would you like a piece?" Blaze asked in the friendliest way he could. "It's prairie dog."

Young Derskin hesitated, and then nodded yes.

Blaze grabbed the biggest piece of meat he had and untied it from his waist strap. With a very warm smile, he reached to hand the slab of meat to Derskin. The boy pointed his arrow slightly to the side as he was receiving the food.

At that instant, Blaze drove his fist into the boy's stomach. His young foe gasped, dropping the bow and arrow from his hand, and staggered backwards. Blaze followed with a second blow, knocking the boy to the ground. Quickly grabbing his knife back from the boy's waist strap, Blaze kneeled over the young Hohokam and held the blade to the boy's throat.

Fear and defiance raged in the Hohokam's eyes. Blaze needed to get away and to find Stonah, but what would he do with Derskin?

With a knife at his throat, Derskin did not move. Blaze could kill him easily, but if he did, he could never be a Hohokam. And an act like that might even start a war between the Hohokam and the Sinaguas. While Blaze was no longer a Sinagua, they were the people of his family, and they were a tribe unprepared for war.

"I wish you no harm," Blaze said.

"That is a strange thing to say holding a knife at my throat."

Blaze pulled his blade back a little.

"If I ask you to stay here until the sun goes down, would you do that?" Blaze asked.

"You know that I couldn't. I would be shamed. If you leave, I must follow. I have already failed. Gratewat will be angry with me."

"Then I must kill you! Is it not better to do as I say?"

"Bravegart will kill me if I let you go."

"Bravegart?"

"Bravegart hates you. He has sworn revenge against Blaze of the Great Cliff. I saw what you did to him. He shamed his pod because of you."

"You were there?"

"Yes. Your Setting Sun went home with a bag full of my beads that day, but you robbed Bravegart of much more."

"Because we beat him?"

"No, there can be honor in defeat. You caused him to hold himself ahead of the pod. His father has refused to let him compete until after the coming winter."

Bravegart was not allowed to play guayball? Because of what happened at that game?

"Please stay here, Derskin."

"I cannot."

Blaze grabbed the boy's neck with his left hand, and pulled his head up, then slammed it down on the hard ground below. When the boy's eyes closed, Blaze leaned over and saw that his chest still moved up and down. His breathing was slow, but he was alive. Thank the Spirit of the Corn, Blaze thought.

As he got to his feet, he heard footsteps rushing up from behind him. He instantly turned, wielding his knife in front of him.

It was Shinestah! A look of horror flashed on her face.

"Blaze, what did you do to Derskin?" she asked with alarm.

Blaze lowered his knife and said, "He is all right. I needed to get away. I asked him to stay here, and he told me that he could not. I did what I needed to do. He should be fine."

Shinestah nodded nervously.

"What are you doing here?" Blaze asked.

"What are *you* doing here?"

Blaze did not answer. He could not answer. Instead, he asked, "Where is Stonah? Why was I captured?"

"Oh, Blaze," Shinestah said kindly, "there is trouble. My people have sent a war party to attack your people. One of your tribesman stole back game from us before you left. Our tribal elders looked at that as an act of war."

"One deer was taken back. And it was ours anyway!"

"It is not just about the deer. There are many who eye your good land and the water at your well. They were looking for a reason to attack. They know from their travels that your people have given up the ways of war. Oh, Blaze, I was so worried that you would die in the fight."

At that moment, Blaze wished that he had been born a Hohokam, like Shinestah. Then he could stay here with her. But he was not Hohokam. He was Sinagua, and his people were in trouble.

"When did they leave for the Great Cliff?" Blaze asked.

"Three days ago."

Curses! He would not be able to get back to his home before the Hohokam attacked.

"How did you know I was here?" Blaze asked.

"Gratewat told Running Bull. Running Bull knew that you were a friend of Stonah's. Because Stonah is was not here, he told me. He knew that we were friends."

Blaze's heart jumped when she said the word *friend*. Shinestah *was* his friend. But his heart felt torn as he looked upon the beautiful, dark haired Hohokam girl. Her kind and lively dark eyes had captivated him when he had first met her. He now knew that her eyes mirrored her kind soul.

"Gratewat went to tell our tribal elders. They will be coming for you soon."

"Where is Stonah? Is he okay?"

"They made him go to Sinagua. He is on his way to fight your people."

"Not Stonah! He never would!"

"He had no choice. He was sick over it, but he had to go. After all, he is Hohokam."

"You are Hohokam, too, yet you tell me all these things. Why?"

"If I could capture you, I would," Shinestah said sadly. "I, too, am Hohokam, but my heart is filled with joy that you hold that arrow, and not me. Otherwise, I could not let you go. Please, save yourself."

"I will."

"Blaze, what are you doing here?"

Blaze did not know what to say. He was ashamed of his reason for coming. He could not confess the truth even to her.

"I cannot say, but it gives me joy to see you one more time."

"As I am glad to see you. I hope that our paths cross again, and our people are at peace."

"Shinestah, I will seek that out."

"Go now, Blaze of the Great Cliff. I will always remember you."

Blaze saw tears roll down Shinestah's face. He felt tears well up behind his own eyes. There was so much he felt but could not say.

"Go!" Shinestah cried. "They will be back here soon!"

Blaze reached out and touched her soft, dark hand. He bowed to her, turned and ran off.

CHAPTER 23

▼

Blaze ran hard in the direction of his home. He needed to return before it was too late. While their cliff dwelling was designed to hold off a much larger enemy force, after countless harvests of peace, many of his tribesmen had become less attentive when on lookout duty. Climbers, too, were less careful, not always calling out their movement up and down the ladders. The Sinagua people might fall quickly if their guards were not alert. If Setting Sun were involved in a game of chance, the whole Hohokam tribe could pass him by unnoticed! At least the lookout guards had been more attentive after Blaze and his traveling party had returned from their recent journey. Blaze prayed to Father Sun that his people had continued their heightened state of alert.

Blaze was certain that if he ran hard the whole way, he could complete the journey by the following day. He had meat in his belly, and more to eat in his food pouch. He had water in his bag, and he felt sure of the way back to his home.

His plan depended on finding water on the journey home. If he walked, and traveled only in the cooler mornings and evenings, then he was sure that he could stretch his water supply until he got to familiar land, land where he knew every creek and spring. But that would add an extra three days to his journey, and those additional days might be the difference in the survival of his people.

No, Blaze decided to run hard all day and into the night as long as Father Sun and the Night Spirits of Light allowed him to see. He would trust Father Spirit to lead him to water. If he did not find it, he would probably die, but that would be a fair punishment for his great sin. He had abandoned his people in their time of greatest need.

Blaze ran. Under a strong late day sun, he took regular sips from his water bag. He drank just enough to enable himself to keep running hard. Blaze headed to the gap between two distant brown hills, which were turning redder as the sun dropped.

When night finally arrived, Blaze crumbled in exhaustion. He wet his mouth with the last drops of water, and reached for another piece of meat. That food would sustain him for his long run the next day. If Blaze could get to familiar territory by nightfall, he would be able to refill his water bag and make his way home in the dark. He needed to find water during the day, though. He could never run the whole day without it. Praying to the Great Spirit for his help, Blaze fell into a deep sleep.

The next thing he heard was the music of the morning birds as the long, warm fingers of Father Sun gently nudged him awake. Blaze ate a small piece of dark meat from his pouch, struggling to force it down his dry throat. Then, he was off.

He ran hard. Harder than he had ever run. He thought back to that long run from his village, when he had hoped and expected his animal spirit would come to him. He ran even harder now. The lives of his people depended on it. He prayed that he would not confront a Hohokam. If he did, his skills as a warrior would be put to the test. He was not sure what he would do when he arrived at his cliff home, but he knew that he must be there to help in any way he could.

Blaze's mouth was an oven of dryness and fire burned in his lungs, yet still, he pushed himself to run even faster. He was determined to get in more distance before the midday heat. Focusing through his sweat-filled eyes, he thought he saw a rippling movement between two distant cliffs. Was it water? Desperately needing to drink, he pushed himself to get there quickly. He ran towards the wavelike movement, which he prayed was water. Yet the more he ran, the further off those ripples seemed to be.

Blaze stopped and squinted ahead, studying the landscape before him. He knew the heat of the desert can play tricks on the eyes. It looked like water he was seeing. Was it an illusion? If the water was real then why did he not get closer to it? Blaze felt almost certain that what he saw was nothing more than heat waves rising from the hot sand. But maybe it was water. It *had* to be water.

Blaze ran again. He ignored his overwhelming thirst and pain, and instead thought about his mother and father and sisters. He thought about his grandfather, and Setting Sun, too, and pictured them under attack. Why had it taken a war for him to realize how much his family and his people meant to him? He was angry with himself and felt shame, but he was determined as well. Determined to make things right, for himself and his people. He reached deep inside himself to run even harder. As the bright sun almost blinded him, his legs no longer felt the earth below his feet. The world was a blur, but Blaze told himself that he had to keep going. He had to do it for his people.

In the midst of the blur before him, two tiny green specks appeared. Glimmering like polished pieces of emerald, they floated above the distant horizon, becoming larger as he moved forward. Feeling almost weightless, each step became easier. As the green lights grew, black dots appeared in the middle. They seemed familiar. What were they?

And then he knew. They were the eyes of his mountain lion! Shimmering with life, they grew bigger and bigger. Blaze continued to move his legs forward over what felt like groundless terrain, while the eyes before him grew bigger and closer still. Fear enveloped him. It almost strangled him, but he kept running.

The two eyes of the lion suddenly filled his entire vision and then melted into one. Even the blacks of the eyes merged, becoming one. The black was like a deep hole, blacker than any black Blaze had ever seen. Blacker than the emery figurines the Anasazi traded or the spar necklaces made by the Mogollons. Blacker than the darkest night. And Blaze was running into the blackness. He was drowning in the blackness. He could not breathe, but he would not give up. He kept his legs moving forward. He felt himself being swallowed by the surrounding darkness, and then there was nothing.

CHAPTER 24

▼

Blaze awoke to the feel of hard rock beneath him and a blanket of heat above. He struggled to open his eyes. The desert was still a blur. Working to focus his vision, he saw the same rippling he had seen earlier, except the ripples were nearly in front of him.

Not able to stand, Blaze crawled forward. He reached for what looked like water, sure that he would touch more hot sand. He let his hand drop into the rippling pool. Wetness! The sensation jolted him to life. His hand was in water! Water! Blaze crawled a body's length forward and put his face into the pool of warm liquid. He sucked it into his mouth and swallowed. He drank and drank, stopping only when sickness began to well up inside him. He held his face in the water, and let it wet his lips and eyes. He savored one of the great gifts of life. Water.

Was he in the Great Underground, or was he still alive? Blaze lifted his head out of the water, and examined his arms and legs. It *was* his body! He was still alive! But what had happened? How had he found the water?

And then he remembered. It was those eyes, the eyes of the mountain lion, and he understood. Blaze had run harder than he had ever run, and his animal spirit had at last come to him. He now knew why it had not come before. The spirit of the mountain lion had waited until he was committed to his people, and not just to himself and his own individual destiny. And then that fierce hunter's spirit came to him when his need was greatest. His animal spirit had guided him to the water.

Blaze was now sure that he would make it back to his people. The mountain lion was part of him. He was no longer a boy, but a man of the Sinagua people.

When his stomach sickness had passed, Blaze drank more water and ate his last piece of meat. Then he stood to continue his journey home. He had fallen as a boy and risen as a man. Blaze filled his water bag, and walked towards the Great Cliff. There was no need to hurry. He would not approach his home without the cloak of darkness to protect him. He also needed to conserve his strength.

As Blaze neared Sinagua land, the sun was still three fists high in the sky. He found a sheltered corner at the base of a small cliff and decided that it would be a good spot to wait. He shut his eyes, hoping to sleep a little. An all-important night awaited him. He needed to be ready.

When his eyes next opened, he was surrounded by darkness. In familiar land, Blaze could travel easily by night. A sliver of moon floated low in the hazy night sky. That was good. It would be easier to remain hidden. He would surely see his first Hohokam warriors at any time. Unless they had already captured the Great Cliff. Blaze shuddered as he thought about the revenge that an angry Bravegart might exact from his people.

Crouching low to the ground, Blaze let his soft hunter's feet take him over the hard ground. With his right hand, he gripped a rough wooden club he had shaped from the branch of a sycamore tree, while his left hand held his bow. Soon he would be at the base of the trail leading to the ladders. Blaze stopped and waited for the slight moon to drop behind the dark shadow that he knew was his cliff home. He prayed that it still *was* his home.

The night's haze dimmed the light from the stars. With almost no moonlight, it was hard to see anything, but the faint shadows and the feel of the familiar land made moving for Blaze as easy as if it were midday.

A sound suddenly broke the silence of the night. It was a voice! A human voice! Blaze stopped and studied each outline in the landscape before him. Moundlike shadows sprinkled the open land ahead and to the right. They must be tents. Hohokam tents! That meant that the enemy had not taken the Great Cliff! He was not too late!

He wondered if the Hohokam would have a guard posted his way. They would certainly be protecting themselves from their cliff side, but would they also protect their plain side? Blaze had to assume that there was a lookout ahead.

How would he approach? There were two trails leading to the cliff's base, one from the creek ahead and one along the face of the cliff leading to the first ledge. With the Hohokam camp at the foot of the creek trail, Blaze would try to get to the other trail, the ledge trail. As quietly as he could, Blaze moved to his left, circling the camp. He guessed where the Hohokam guards might be, and steered as wide of those spots as possible.

Approaching the ledge trail, Blaze scanned the darkness ahead while straining his ears to pick up the slightest sound. There was nothing at first. Then he thought he heard something! It sounded like an animal or a man chewing. Slowly and even more quietly, Blaze stepped forward. Ahead, he detected the shadow of a figure perched on a ledge. It looked like a second person was next to him. As Blaze approached, he realized there definitely was another body next to the sitting figure. They must be guards, Blaze thought. It looked as if the second guard was lying down. He was probably sleeping.

Blaze trusted his skill with the bow, and knew that he could shoot the guard sitting up. He had never killed a person, but he was not afraid to do so now. Blaze had been trained as a warrior by his grandfather, and a warrior defends his home against invaders. Then a scary thought came to him. What if the guard was Stonah? Blaze suddenly felt sick He was not so sure he could shoot the shadowed figure before him. Besides, if Blaze did shoot the guard, he would probably call out and wake his fellow tribesman.

I need a plan, Blaze thought. If he could get past those two warriors guarding the ledge trail, then he could climb to his dwelling and maybe get everyone out before the other Hohokam knew it. His people could even attack the invaders. A surprise attack at night might succeed. But would the ladders still be there? Blaze needed to get to the cliff to find out.

Soundlessly, Blaze approached the seated figure. From the size of him, the guard appeared to be a boy. Was it Stonah? Or was it Braveg-art? Blaze tightened his grip on his club as he stepped within striking distance. The smooth hard rock below allowed Blaze to move in silence. Breathing with the wind, he glided forward and swung his club towards the head. Crack! The guard slumped to the ground, making a quiet thud as he struck the rock. He lay face up among the shadows as Blaze struggled to identify him. It was a young man that Blaze did not recognize. He could have been one of the men in the guayball game Blaze had watched, but it was too dark to be sure.

The sleeping figure rustled. Blaze pulled his club back and prepared to strike. The Hohokam turned and Blaze recognized him! It was Stonah!

Stonah tried to call out when Blaze pressed the palm of his hand over his friend's mouth. Stonah's eyes widened in panic and then must have recognized Blaze as he instantly calmed down.

"Will you be quiet?" Blaze asked.

Stonah nodded 'yes.'

Blaze knew that he could trust the boy. Honor was one of the highest virtues with all the peoples of the earth. And besides, this was Stonah, his friend.

"What happened?" Blaze whispered quietly.

"We tried to attack the first day, but big clubs came from the doors and drove two of our warriors off the ledge of your cliff. They died.

Another was hurt when your people pushed over a ladder he was climbing."

"Were other ladders knocked down"? Blaze asked.

"No. We did not try to climb them again."

"Did Bravegart die?" Blaze asked in a hushed voice.

"No, but they were two men from the West Village."

"Will you attack again?" Blaze asked.

Stonah looked into the eyes of his friend, but said nothing. Blaze understood. He could not ask his friend to betray his own people.

Finally, Stonah whispered quietly, "How did you escape?"

"I was not in the cliff. I was traveling to your land. I just returned."

"Another journey there so soon?" Stonah asked.

"No, I..." Blaze hesitated. How could he tell Stonah that he had wanted to become a Hohokam? The Hohokam were now at war with his people.

"You found out that we had attacked?" Stonah asked.

Blaze nodded. "I must help my people. Can I ask you to lay here quietly?"

Stonah paused, and said, "What would I say to my people? How could I live with them afterwards? How could I go home if your men came down and slaughtered my sleeping brothers? You know that I cannot do that."

"Yet you do not call out."

"I told you I wouldn't. But I cannot stand and allow you to bring your people down this trail. And I cannot remain silent much longer."

"I understand," Blaze said and nodded. He then ripped a piece of Stonah's breechcloth away, rolled it into a ball and stuffed it into his friend's mouth. He pulled the rope from Stonah's waist, and tied it around the boy's head, tightening it and forcing the cloth deeper into his mouth. As Stonah squirmed, his remaining piece of breechcloth fell to the ground. Blaze picked up the cloth and covered his friend's mid-section with it and then grabbed the lash from the other Hohokam's waist. With that, Blaze tied Stonah's wrists together behind him, then pulled his feet back, and fastened them to his tied hands. At last, Blaze was sure that Stonah would be unable to either move or call out.

"I'm sorry, my friend," Blaze said, and quietly made his way up the dark ledge. It was a walk he had made countless times, and he knew exactly where his tribesmen would be. The first room was the guard house. There would surely be two or three Sinaguas armed with poles and spears, prepared to drive any invaders off the ledge. Blaze cautiously approached the first opening. He knew that his people would not step out and expose themselves. They would wait until he was further up and more vulnerable.

As Blaze stepped within an arm's length of the guard room opening, he stopped and whispered ever so quietly, "Blaze prepared to enter the first ledge."

Silence. Blaze tried to imagine himself in the guard room, expecting an attack. He would surely suspect a trick and never stick his head out. What could he say now to convince his people that it really was him? An idea came to him.

He repeated, "Blaze prepared to enter the first ledge." He paused and added, "And if it's Setting Sun, and you don't believe me, I'll wager three arrow heads to one of your foolish beads that it really is me."

At once, two eyes peeked out around the ledge. In the darkness, Blaze struggled to see who the guard was. From the shape of her head, Blaze instantly knew. It was his sister! It was Bay Leaf!

"Blaze!" she whispered.

A second face appeared in the shadows. It was Great Bear, the Chief Elder!

Blaze quickly stepped inside the guard room.

"Blaze, where were you?" Bay Leaf asked. "We were so worried, and many of the elders were so angry. Why—"

"We do not have time for idle talk," Great Bear interrupted. "How did you get up here? Are the Hohokam still guarding both trails?"

"Chief Elder, there were two Hohokam braves guarding the ledge trail. I have knocked one out and tied up the other. They will both be quiet for a while. I did not see a guard at the creek trail, but I stayed a distance away. I assume that there are at least two guards there. One Hohokam is guarding the rear of their camp near the creek. The rest are sleeping in tents. It looks like there are about twenty or thirty warriors altogether."

Great Bear nodded.

Blaze looked at his sister and the Chief Elder, and said, "Forgive me for asking, but why is it that a young girl and a village elder are guarding the ledge in time of war?"

"All the men were sent off on a hunting expedition," Great Bear said. "Our food was too low. We would not have survived the cold winter season. They have headed toward Anasazi land. We had heard of fighting there, and so we sent all our young men, leaving grand elders, women and children at the cliff."

"They think that all of our people are still here in the cliff," Blaze said. "We must escape before first light!"

"We cannot escape, Blaze."

"Why not, Chief Elder?"

"Our oldest and youngest could not move away quickly enough. The Hohokam would catch up with us."

"But we must do something! When first light arrives, they will discover what I did to their guards, and our escape route will be cut off again."

"You are right, we must do something. I shall seek counsel."

Great Bear stood and left the room.

"Oh, Blaze," Bay Leaf cried, "Mother has been so upset. They said that you ran off! Mother said that you would never do such a thing, and that you must have had an accident. She was sure that you were hurt or dead. Where were you?"

The words got stuck in his throat. What could he say.

"Blaze, tell me! Where were you? What happened?"

Blaze hesitated, and finally spoke. "Bay Leaf, I am sorry. I did leave. It was a child's foolish idea, but that child is gone, and a Sinagua man has returned. A man possessed with the great spirit of the mountain lion."

"Your spirit came to you?"

Blaze nodded. "And I am sorry for the pain that I have caused you and the rest of my family and tribe. I will use all my skill as a warrior to aid my people now in their time of need."

"I am glad that you are back," Bay Leaf said, stepping forward and hugging her brother. "Chittanberry will be very happy, too. She has been so sad since you have been gone. And mother. Blaze, you don't know how sad she has been. She never smiles and barely eats. She hardly pays any attention to little Chittanberry. I feel like Chittanberry is my child now. Oh, mother will be so relieved. I must go tell her! Keep guard, Blaze."

"Wait. Is Setting Sun here, or with the men?"

"He is here. Some of the older boys remained here at the cliff."

Blaze was happy to hear that. As Bay Leaf was leaving, Blaze's grandfather entered with Great Bear and two other grand elders, Golden Eagle and Swift Arrow.

"Grandfather!" Blaze cried.

Lion Heart bowed respectfully to Blaze.

Blaze and Great Bear explained the situation to the other grand elders. When they were finished talking, the old men sat speechless for a long time. A wise elder ponders matters thoroughly before offering an opinion.

Finally, Blaze's grandfather spoke. "Blaze," Lionheart said, "you must travel to the men of our tribe and tell them what has happened. If the Hohokam think that all of our people are up here, then we will have the advantage of a surprise attack on them. Even though we will be outnumbered and confronting a people better trained in the art of war, we might be able to defeat them. A surprise attack at night is what I suggest."

There was silence as each man considered the idea. The other grand elders knew that Great Bear did not like to fight, and so they looked to him for his opinion of Lion Heart's plan.

Great Bear nodded, and said, "I agree. Blaze should go. He is young and strong, and can travel quickly. He is also capable of defending himself. But he must get away without any Hohokam knowing it. If he leaves, the young boy Stonah will know that he has gone. I see that we have no choice but to kill the boy. That way, the rest will not know that Blaze has escaped."

Kill Stonah? Blaze felt a deep pain in his heart. He did not know if he could do that! Silence filled the room for a moment.

"Wait," Lion Heart finally said. "Killing Stonah will do no good. When they find him dead, they will assume that many or all of our people escaped. They will be even more alert for an attack. We need the Hohokam boy alive, so he can tell his people that only one Sinagua, just one boy, escaped. After we give Blaze a little time to travel some distance away, we will start to move others out of the cliff, making only enough noise to awaken some of their sleeping warriors. Then, we will retreat back to our dwellings, and the Hohokam will think that only one boy got away and that they stopped the rest of us. They will not worry about an attack from one young boy. Yes, I think that we need to keep the Hohokam boy alive."

Blaze's heart leapt with joy, but he held his breath, too. Would Great Bear and the other elders agree?

"You are right," Great Bear said. "Blaze, you will go."

"Go?" Lightfoot cried as she ran into room.

Seeing his mother's face and hearing her cry of alarm made Blaze sick with sorrow and regret.

"My son just returns and now he must go?" Anger and disbelief rang from her voice.

"It is necessary for the survival of our people," Great Bear spoke solemnly.

Saying nothing, Lightfoot turned and rested her eyes on her son. Blaze could not tell if she was happy or sad.

"Mother," Blaze finally said, and moved towards her.

At that moment, Lightfoot stepped forward and hugged her son. She squeezed Blaze so hard that he could barely breathe. When he was sure that she would release him, she kept right on squeezing him. Blaze thought about the spirits of his brothers buried within the wall of their fourth floor dwelling, and he knew that his mother must have believed that she had lost the last of her sons as well. How could he have thought to leave his people? And just to play a game! The pain she had suffered had all been his fault. He was a man now, and he vowed to himself that he would never again cause her pain. He would live his life to make her proud.

"Lightfoot," Great Bear said, "he must go now. He will return. I know it."

Finally, Lightfoot released Blaze and stepped back. Her face was covered with her tears.

"Perhaps you should not travel alone," Great Bear said to Blaze. "It is too important, and you will be safer with a companion. Setting Sun is also young and strong. He will go with you."

"But the Hohokam boy will see him," Golden Eagle said.

"The Hohokam will still not be concerned about only two boys," Great Bear answered. "Bay Leaf, awake Setting Sun. Tell him to prepare to travel."

Blaze's sister nodded, and went out. In moments, Setting Sun was entering the small room behind Bay Leaf. He was carrying his bow and arrow, and had a food pouch attached to his waist strap. Setting Sun beamed with joy when he saw Blaze.

The elders handed Setting Sun bags of food and water as they quickly explained what he had to do. Setting Sun nodded.

"Be off!" Great Bear commanded. "Move swiftly. Our food and water supplies on the cliff will not last forever."

Blaze nodded to his people. He could not look at his mother, though. He could not bear to see her pain. Quickly he turned around and was gone.

CHAPTER 25

▼

Avoiding the eyes of his tied-up friend, Blaze pulled Setting Sun past Stonah and his unconscious companion. Bound so tightly, Stonah must have been very uncomfortable, but it was necessary that he not escape.

"But—" Setting Sun said.

"Sh!" Blaze hushed, yanking his friend past Stonah's squirming body.

He led the way down the ledge path, praying that the Hohokam would not hear the brushing of Setting Sun's feet along the ground. Setting Sun had never learned to walk with the soft feet of a hunter. To Blaze, every shuffle of his friend's yucca sandals against the ground seemed to echo through the night.

Blaze wondered if he should slow down, and maybe Setting Sun would make less noise. Or should he travel more quickly, assuming that the Hohokam will hear him anyway, and at least they would be further along in their escape?

The element of surprise would be critical in any attack on these people. If the Hohokam suspected that many of the men had escaped, they would certainly guard their rear more heavily. But Stonah would tell them that only Blaze and Setting Sun had gotten away.

Blaze and Setting Sun were nearly out of the Hohokam camp when they heard a sound and stopped in their tracks.

"Over there!" a man's voice called out in that familiar Hohokam way of speaking.

Blaze froze. Setting Sun stood equally still as footsteps began to approach. Blaze slowly and quietly slipped an arrow onto his bow, and drew it back as far as he could pull. Three shadowed figures emerged from around a boulder below. Blaze aimed his arrow at the first figure. He was sure that he could hit him, and maybe have enough time to load another arrow and fire before one of the companions was upon him. But he could never get the third, and so he aimed a little higher, turning his bow slightly to the right, and released his arrow.

An instant later, Blaze heard his stone arrowhead strike the rocky ledge to the left of the three Hohokam.

"There!" a voice called, and all three figures ran towards the area where the arrow had hit the ledge.

"Let's go!" Blaze whispered to Setting Sun, remaining low to the ground as they ran. Their pattering footsteps were lost in the sounds of the Hohokam people calling out to one another.

At the bottom of the trail, Blaze and Setting Sun made their way through the brush and trees surrounding the dried up river bank. Even in the black of night, Blaze and Setting Sun knew every rock, root and shrub, and could move through this land as if it were midday. The Hohokam would be slowed by the darkness.

Just as the two boys pulled out of the wooded area and into open ground, the first brightness of Father Sun lit the distant sky to their right.

"No!" Blaze cursed. "We'll never reach the hills before they see us. Should we hide or run?"

Setting Sun pursed his lips and put his hand to his mouth, exactly as he did when calculating the chances in one of his wagering games.

"We have to run," Setting Sun declared. "Otherwise they will know that we could not have escaped. They will look until they find us."

"We could hide in the tool storage cave," Blaze suggested.

"For how long?" Setting Sun asked in a way that suggested the answer.

Blaze knew that his friend was right. The Hohokam could wait forever, but he and Setting Sun would quickly run out of water and food.

"Okay," Blaze said decisively. "Let's go!"

Blaze led the way, running hard across the dry plain. The sky brightened from a dark blue to pink, and then the first rays from Father Sun shone over the distant hills. They heard no sound from behind. Maybe they would escape unseen!

Blaze could run harder but felt Setting Sun falling back. He slowed his pace a little until his friend was up with him again.

"We need to go faster!" Blaze pleaded.

Setting Sun nodded.

The hills ahead were getting closer. If only they could get there without being seen! As Blaze sprinted, the tortured look on Setting Sun's face made it clear that he was pushing himself as hard as he could. They moved past the bear boulder to their left and ran right towards the giant double saguaro cactus, which had been the site of many childhood games. The great cactus had always been a two-headed monster to both Blaze and Setting Sun. It was now a merciful protector inviting them to the safety of the hills beyond.

Blaze lunged past the cactus and fell to the ground. Setting Sun stumbled to the dirt just behind him. They were past the plain. They could no longer be seen from the hills of the cliff! They had made it!

And then Blaze turned around and looked back towards the Great Cliff. In the distance, he spotted a band of Hohokam heading their way!

"Curses!" Blaze swore. "They must have seen us!"

Setting Sun nodded.

"Let's go!" Blaze commanded.

The two boys ran around the hill to the flatter land on the other side. They would have to keep ahead of their pursuers for the day. If they remained uncaught until nightfall, then they could move undetected in the dark and might escape.

Blaze ran, but was careful not to pull too far ahead of his friend. He could hear Setting Sun's heavy breathing. Blaze knew that he could easily outrun the Hohokam men trailing him, but he did not think that Setting Sun could.

For the first time, the thought of leaving Setting Sun behind crept into his head. How could he leave his friend alone to face the enemy? Yet it was essential that he find his tribesmen and warn them, otherwise all his people could die.

Setting Sun collapsed to the hard ground.

"You go," he said to Blaze. "You need to go alone. I can't do this."

"How can I leave you here? They'll get you!"

"Blaze, if you stay, they will get us both."

"Probably, but I'll take some of them down first."

"But what about the rest of our people? You know that you must think of them first. Do your duty. I will be fine. When you return, you can rescue me, just like you always did when we played as children."

Blaze smiled as he recalled the war games he had played as a boy. And then he turned his thoughts back to the decision that he needed to make. He knew that he must go, but he did not want Setting Sun captured by the Hohokam. Not alone, and not by Bravegart.

"They won't capture you!" Blaze said. "You will hide."

"They will find me. As you said, I cannot remain in hiding too long."

Blaze searched the landscape ahead. His eyes were drawn to the low lying cliffs far off to their right.

"Moving over that stony ground will leave no trail," Blaze said. "You can hide behind those rocks over there."

"But that's the only place anyone could hide around here. They'll surely look there."

"They won't if they are following the two of us in another direction."

"But they'll see just one person in the distance."

"I will make my trail look like there are two of us running. They won't even look for you!"

Setting Sun's eyes opened wide. "Great idea! But won't they see just one person?"

"Not if the distance is great enough. I must leave now, Setting Sun. Trust me."

"Where will we meet?" Setting Sun asked.

"On the other side of Squirrel Hill. Wait until you can safely travel. Move by night if you can. I will see you soon."

"Blaze, if I am not there tomorrow by midday, go on without me."

A wave of sadness welled up in Blaze's chest, but he nodded to his friend.

"Don't look so worried," Setting Sun said. "We'll make it. I'll be there in a day."

Blaze gave his friend a nervous nod.

"I'd bet on it," Setting Sun said with a smile.

Blaze smiled back and held out his hand to the boy he knew better than anyone in the world.

As they clasped hands, they peered deeply into each other's eyes. The two boys were one, and they did not want to break that bond.

"My brother," Blaze thought, and then turned to leave.

CHAPTER 26

▼

Blaze could feel the heat of the late morning sun draining the energy from his body, but he continued to push ahead. The Hohokam would be getting to the hill any time. Blaze hoped that his trail was marked heavily enough to lead his enemy past Setting Sun's hiding place, but he had been careful not to overdo it. If the signs of his trail were too obvious, some smart Hohokam might suspect a trick.

Blaze turned around to see if he could detect any pursuers. There were none. Still, Blaze worried that when they got to the hill, they would be close enough to see just one person running. If that happened, then they would search for Setting Sun and surely find him.

Blaze searched for something to make it look as if there were two people running. He spotted a prickly pear cactus ahead. He ran to the spiny bush and grabbed his knife. He put the blade to the base of the cactus and, with a sawing motion, began cutting through it. As soon as he had cut the cactus free, Blaze untied his breechcloth and used extra rope from the tie to attach the cactus to his side. The needles dug into his bare skin, but he did not have time to cut them away. Blaze felt confident that, from a distance, it would look as if two people were running. He was also sure that if he ran his hardest, he could increase the distance between himself and his pursuers, making it even harder for them to see that his companion was not a boy but a cactus.

As Blaze ran, his calves and thighs pleaded for rest. Still, he continued to run hard. Blaze ran through the pain until he seemed to feel nothing, but his legs still pushed him onward. He felt himself being swallowed into the spirit of his mountain lion once again. This time, he was not afraid. He felt only the comfort and safety of his spirit protector.

By the time he reached the Mescal Cliffs, he realized that he could go no further. He collapsed at the watering hole around the north ridge, and was relieved to see that it was not completely dried up. He put his face into the warm brown liquid, and sucked it through his parched lips. It was so good!

Blaze drank his fill, and then sat down. It was the first time he had rested in a long time. As the throbbing in his legs lessened, he began to feel the sting of the cactus needles cutting into his bare skin. Earlier, his side had numbed to the pain, but feeling was beginning to return. He untied the cactus and pulled it away. Fresh streams of bright red blood ran down his side over the black dirt and the dried brown blood caking his skin. After hiding the bloodied cactus behind a boulder, Blaze arose and headed towards Squirrel Hill, where he prayed that he would rejoin Setting Sun the next day.

After a long night and morning, Blaze at last arrived to his rendezvous point, but Setting Sun was nowhere to be found. Had he been captured? Or was he still hiding? Blaze thought that if he waited another day, Setting Sun might come along.

But he knew that he could not wait. The survival of his people came first. It came before his own safety and that of his friend or any individual in his tribe. He could not erase the image of his friend from his mind. Blaze could see the smiling face of Setting Sun throwing his bone dice and proudly declaring himself a winner once again. He pictured Setting Sun calculating betting odds, or just laughing. With a heavy heart, Blaze arose, bid farewell to his absent friend, and headed north towards Anasazi land.

Blaze was tempted to run and reach his people as soon as possible, but he needed to travel wisely, and preserve his water. If Blaze failed to find the men of his tribe, then the Hohokam would surely wait out the Sinaguas at the cliff, and capture the women, children and elders when they finally came down to replenish their water. If that happened, the Hohokam would know that the Sinagua men had gone, and they would wait to slaughter them on their return home. Without the cliff for protection or the element of surprise, any battle would be a disaster for Sinagua men so untrained in fighting ways.

Moving into new territory beyond Squirrel Hill, Blaze was not afraid. He knew that he should reach a river within a day. If he followed that river, he would be taken to the canyon lands, which is where his people had probably gone to hunt.

Blaze traveled quickly across the dry plains, sipping regular amounts of water. As the sun moved towards its resting spot beneath the horizon, Blaze picked up his pace even more. He ate small bits of meat from his food pouch to keep up his strength, and kept moving forward.

When day ended and he could see no more, he stopped. The cool air of the desert night felt good. He lay his sore body down on a bed of soft desert moss and was soon asleep.

The next thing he knew, the warmth of the morning sun was gently drawing him from the world of dreams. Blaze put a piece of meat into his mouth, and washed it down with a small sip of water. He then grabbed his bow and was off. Just before midday, he scanned the horizon and saw green in the distance! It had to be the river! The river meant water to drink, and a path leading to his people. Blaze prayed that his eyes were not tricking him.

As the surrounding plant life grew more abundant, he knew that his eyes had not deceived him. Before long, Blaze was kneeling at the edge of a tree-lined river. Actually, it was more like a creek, with the water moving at barely a trickle, but it was water. Blaze gorged himself with the clear liquid. After, he refilled his water bag and then moved northward, keeping the river to his right.

For much of the afternoon, Blaze trotted along the winding bank of the river. As the sun dropped lower in the western sky, Blaze knew he had to replenish his supply of food. He had passed small game throughout the day, but he had not taken the time to hunt. Needing to eat for the strength to continue, Blaze scoured the land ahead for any movement. He saw nothing.

After advancing a few tree lengths further, Blaze was drawn toward a rustling sound behind a cluster of yucca bushes. Quietly and quickly, he approached. With drawn bow, he neared the shaking branches, and then the movement stopped. It was probably a big animal, judging from the sound. Suddenly, out scurried a small rabbit. Blaze drew back his arrow, aimed and fired. The rabbit fell. That small creature never could have made the noise I heard, Blaze thought. Then from the same bush came another arrow. It skittered off a nearby rock. It was followed by a scrawny, dirty-faced boy.

"I got it!" he cried, running to the rabbit. Blaze guessed that the boy must have been eight or nine harvests of age.

Blaze did not move as the thin child ran up to the rabbit and reached down to pull his arrow out of the dead animal. As he put his small hands on the arrow shaft, the child froze. He must be realizing that it is not his arrow, Blaze thought.

And then the boy's eyes opened wide in panic as he looked up and saw Blaze standing nearby with a drawn bow. Instantly, he turned and ran.

"Stop!" Blaze called.

The boy continued to run. Blaze sprinted after him, and in no time, caught up to him. Blaze grabbed his arm and yelled, "Stop!"

The child stood still and turned to Blaze. He stuck out his jaw and lowered his eyebrows trying to look brave, but his eyes betrayed his terror.

"It's all right," Blaze said kindly. "I'm not going to hurt you."

The young boy eyed Blaze suspiciously but said nothing.

"My name is Blaze. I am a Sinagua."

"From the Great Cliff?"

"Yes."

Instantly the child seemed to relax.

"I am Running River."

"Are you Anasazi?"

The boy nodded.

"From the Great Canyon?"

"No. My family lives in a small village along the river up ahead."

Blaze noticed the familiar swirl to the woven cloth he wore around his waist. He would recognize that pattern anywhere. It was the work of Tall Grass, Setting Sun's father.

"Where did you get that breechcloth?" Blaze asked.

"Your people traded it to me. We exchanged meat and fish for cloth."

"When did you see my people?"

"They were here less than a moon ago."

"Do you know where they went?"

"They were seeking good hunting ground. My elders would know. Come."

"You take the rabbit," Blaze said.

Running River removed Blaze's arrow and handed it back to him. After picking up his own arrow, the young boy turned to the north and started to run.

Jogging slowly, Blaze followed him up the river to a small cluster of adobe homes nestled together near the bank of the river. A handful of women and men were working in the surrounding fields when one of them spotted Blaze with Running River.

"Ayoy!" she cried.

Immediately everyone's attention went to the two boys. The men in the field ahead wore expressions of concern as they ran to Running River and the strange boy.

"Father," Running River said to the first man, "this is Blaze of the Great Cliff."

The long haired man responded with a less worried look, and nodded to Blaze. "I am Black Bear of the southern settlement. We are of the Anasazi tribe."

"I am looking for my people," Blaze said.

"Are you alone?" a second man asked.

Blaze nodded.

"They traveled through here about ten days past."

"Do you know where my people were going?"

"North to the hills," the man spoke, pointing in a direction further up river.

"How will I find those hills?"

"Follow the river for two more days, and then go west when you get to the Great Falls."

"Thank you. I will go now."

"No, you must stay and share bread with us this evening," another man spoke up.

"My people at the cliff are under attack. I must warn my tribesmen and return to aid the rest of my people at home."

"Under attack?" the oldest of the four men asked. "Who has attacked?"

"Hohokam."

The gray haired man nodded. "A band of Hohokam hunters came through here two moons ago. They shot our game but gave us nothing in return."

"I must go," Blaze said.

"No, you must stay and eat. You will need all your strength if you are to travel quickly to the hills. It looks like Running River has added to the evening's stew," he said, eyeing the rabbit the boy was holding.

"No—" the boy began.

"He is a good hunter," Blaze said, interrupting.

Running River flashed a look of pride and gratitude towards Blaze.

"Let me help you in the fields," Blaze said. He hated to work the fields, but how could he stand by waiting to eat while others worked?

Black Bear nodded, and Blaze and Running River stepped into the field to help pick the winter squash. It was a late season variety that was not grown at the Great Cliff.

There seemed to be four families living together in the small cluster of river homes. The four women shortly went in from the fields while the men continued to work alongside two older boys. A handful of children who had been playing near the fields stared at Blaze and giggled among themselves.

Soon, the baskets were filled with squash and the men headed back to their shelter with the fresh produce. Unlike the Sinagua cliff homes or the Hohokam dwellings of stone, the Anasazi houses appeared to be made of mud. Blaze asked Running River about it. The boy told Blaze they were made from a hardened mudlike material called caliche. Along the southern side of each house hung a line of squashes, drying in the sun. Just as at the cliff, dried vegetables and meat would sustain these people in the cold winter months.

Reflecting the setting sun, the caliche was a beautiful skin-colored red. Blaze followed Running River through the main doorway.

Inside the dwelling, conversation was sparse as the families busily prepared for their meal.

"Can I see your arrows?" Running River asked Blaze.

Blaze nodded and handed the younger boy his six arrows.

"Wow!" Running River said as he ran his finger along the smooth shaft and the polished sides of an arrowhead. He then pushed on the sharp tip, drawing his hand back quickly as the point pricked his finger. "These are beautiful! How do you make such perfect arrowheads?"

Blaze smiled as he began to proudly explain the whole process. He started with his search for just the right materials. Running River's wide eyes remained riveted on Blaze as he spoke. At the same time, the smells of fried squash and corn bread and simmering stew meat made Blaze very glad that he had chosen to stay for dinner. And seeing the families working together made him yearn to be back at the Great Cliff with his own family. A sadness crept over him as he wondered if he would ever again be with his mother, sisters, grandfather and even his father. He was more determined than ever to get back home.

CHAPTER 27

▼

Blaze thought he heard a rumble in the distance. Could he be near the waterfalls already? Running River's father had told him that it would take two days to travel there, but Blaze had run nearly the whole way. Doing so, he had discovered that he could run through pain, move beyond it, and then find a rhythm and run forever.

For the third time that day, Blaze felt eyes following him. The riverbank was thick with foliage and could be hiding any number of people. The men from Running River's home did say there were a few small Anasazi settlements along the waterway, but the Anasazi were not a warlike people, and they would avoid conflict. Still, he did not like being watched.

As he ran, the distant rumble slowly grew to a roar. It *had to be* the falls! Blaze turned with the bend in the river and then stood, staring ahead in awe. A tower of water was crashing down an enormous rocky cliff, exploding into a bubbling pool at the bottom. He and Setting Sun and even Spear Thrower used to play under smaller falls near the well back home, but Blaze tried not let his mind think about that. It made him too sad. Instead, he just refilled his water bag and turned left.

Almost immediately, Blaze spotted the tracks of a large group of people moving to the west. Blaze stopped and examined the footprints more carefully. They seemed fairly fresh. Looking even more closely, he recognized the familiar imprint from their yucca sandals. The travelers were definitely his people!

The sun ahead hung low in the late day sky. Blazed wondered if he should remain where he was for the night. It would be too hard to follow the trail without light from Father Sun. He held his hand out at arms length and lined his fingers below the sun. Four fingers separated the sun from the western horizon. There was still time to cover more distance. Blaze quickly moved on.

The tracks were easy to follow. Many people were on the move and no effort had been made to cover up their trail. The day was almost over and Blaze knew that his body needed rest, but he let his mountain lion's spirit push him on.

As the sun touched the rocky hills of the horizon, Blaze let his legs begin to slow down. Aching and exhausted, he staggered to a nearby rock, and collapsed against it. The last of Father Sun was disappearing from the sky. Dropping between two distant hills, a final speck of red light seemed to wink at Blaze, and then the sun disappeared. The fiery ball of light and warmth had retired to its nightly rest. The sky was still a dim blue overhead and pink on the horizon, but very quickly, all traces of color from Father Sun would be gone.

Blaze grabbed his water bag, unfastened the top, and slowly sipped the liquid. Once his tongue was moistened, Blaze reached into his food bag and took a piece of buffalo meat the Anasazi had given him. He thanked the Great Father and the spirit of the great beast that had been killed. The bag bulged to the top with food, and so Blaze let himself eat until his stomach was full. Tomorrow he would find his people. He needed the energy to get to them as soon as possible.

As the sky turned black, Blaze felt strangely at peace. His people were divided and at war, and Setting Sun, if he was alive, was surely in great danger. Yet Blaze believed that the gods below looked kindly upon him. While he knew that it had been wrong to try to leave his people to join another tribe, he also knew that had he not left, there would have been no one to discover that the Hohokam had attacked. There would be no one to run and find the men of his tribe, and save his people trapped at the cliff.

Blaze was no longer a boy trying to find his place in a tribe where he did not seem to fit. Thanks to his animal spirit, he was now a man and a warrior with a people who needed his skills. He was a man who realized that he needed his people, too, as much as they needed him.

The last trace of light in the distant sky was gone. The blackness above was speckled with the countless shimmering white dots from the stars that filled the night sky. The village elders said that for each spirit in the Great Underground, there was a star above. Was Setting Sun up there? Blaze hoped that a new star had not been born that day.

Blaze could barely make out the silhouette of the distant hills against the night sky. He looked at those dark hills where his people were most likely hunting. At that higher ground the vegetation was probably greener and game must be more abundant.

Studying the dark horizon ahead, Blaze noticed a lone star flickering at the foot of one hill. But there shouldn't be a star so low in the sky. Unless it was a new star being born. Was it the star of Setting Sun, beginning its ascent into the night sky? A knot of sickness arose from his stomach and lodged in his throat. Laboring to breathe, he prayed that it was not the star of his friend passing onto the next life.

Blaze studied the star more carefully. It was not as white and clear as the other stars in the sky. It almost had a trace of orange. Like a fire. A fire! Maybe it was a fire! It might be the night fire of his people! Perhaps they were cooking freshly killed game. It must be that! His people must be there, in the hills! Looking harder, Blaze was certain that he was seeing a campfire.

Blaze was sure that he could be at their camp before Father Sun's sleep was half through. But what if they were not his people? He would have to wait until daylight to travel back to where he was now, and pick up the trail of his tribesmen. Unless the people ahead were Anasazi. They might know where the Sinaguas were hunting. But they also might be the Hohokam hunters. Blaze shuddered. If they were Hohokam, he would prefer to approach them at night rather than in the daylight. Yes, he would travel to the fire immediately.

Blaze trembled with nervous excitement as he rose to his feet and started in the direction of the orange twinkle. He let the spirit of the mountain lion fill his soul and he began running. Food and water had given new life to his body, and the thought of his people just ahead had boosted his spirits. The ground moved below his running feet as if he were floating on air.

In a short time, he was approaching the camp. The fire had gotten smaller. If they were his people, they would have finished their cooking. A chill hung in the air, but it was not cold. Still, they would keep a small fire alive through the night so that it would be ready for cooking in the morning.

Blaze moved toward the rocks to his right, and quietly stepped forward, all the time staying low to the ground. Without making a sound, he approached the camp. There would surely be lookouts, but they did not expect an attack and might be less watchful.

His grandfather had taught him how to move like the wind. It was impossible to not make any sound. The aim was to make as little noise as possible, and make sure that those noises blend in with the natural sounds of the area. Blaze approached the fire, and noticed the cocoon-like shapes of men covered by blankets sleeping on the bare ground. He recognized the woven cloth of the blankets and knew at once that these were his people.

Blaze looked up and saw Running Stream perched midway up on a short cliff. He must be the lookout. Was he sleeping? Blaze grabbed a stone and threw it in his direction.

Instantly, Running Stream's tall figure arose as he called out, "Who is there?"

The sleeping bodies on the ground stirred and in a moment the Sinaguas were all on their feet.

"It's me, Blaze!"

"Blaze?"

It was the voice of his father, Swift Deer.

"Yes, Father, it is I," Blaze said as he stepped into a clearing.

"Blaze!" Long Horn said, running up to him. The rest of the tribesmen followed.

"Blaze," Swift Deer said, "how did you get here? What are you doing here?"

"Father, our people are in great danger. The Great Cliff is under attack."

"Under attack?" Running Stream asked. "Who has attacked us?"

"The Hohokam."

"I knew it!" Running Stream said. "I said on our journey that they were a dangerous people, and that we should be wary of them."

"And your actions made them that much more dangerous," Swift Deer said, referring to the deer Running Stream had stolen back.

"They would have found another excuse to attack," Running Stream argued.

"Maybe," Dark Wolf said. "Blaze, have they captured the Great Cliff?"

"No. The Hohokam think that our whole tribe is up there. Almost a moon ago we defended against their first attack, and now they are waiting until we run out of food and water."

"If they knew that the cliff was being defended by women and old men, then they might attack sooner," Swift Deer said.

"Father, my Anasazi friends told me that there were Hohokam hunting in this land," Blaze said. "What if they hear that our men are here and not back at the Great Cliff?"

"Then the Hohokam hunters will go to the cliff and tell their people to attack before we return," Swift Deer said.

No one said a word.

At last, Tall Grass spoke. "How is Setting Sun?" he asked quietly. "Did you see him?"

Blaze began to answer, but hesitated. In his life at the cliff, he had spent almost as much time in Setting Sun's second floor dwelling as he had in his own. When Blaze's father was his most uncaring, Tall Grass had always respected Blaze and made him feel welcome in his home. Tall Grass had treated him like a son. How could he tell this kind man that his youngest son had probably been captured by the Hohokam, or might even be dead?

"Uh," Blaze said, "he was safely in hiding when I last saw him."

"We have no time for idle news," Dark Wolf interrupted. "We must quickly return to the cliff, before it is too late. Let us prepare to travel."

CHAPTER 28

▼

The band of Sinaguas moved quickly through Anasazi land, but after running the entire distance from the cliff, the fast walk back seemed slow to Blaze. A number of times, he found himself at the front of the pack with Long Horn, Running Stream, Sharp Stone and Spear Thrower. All the guayball players. Knowing how important every moment was, it pained him to have to wait for the others.

By the time they stopped for the evening meal, the younger men seemed barely tired while most of the elders pulled up slowly and almost collapsed onto the ground.

"It will take us many days at this pace," Running Stream said to Dark Wolf.

The Sinagua elder nodded.

Blaze knew what Running Stream was suggesting, but it would be disrespectful to propose leaving the elders behind. Silence filled the air as Running Stream's words fell heavily upon each of the older men.

"A day might be the difference in the survival of our people," Swift Deer finally said. "We should send a group ahead."

Dark Wolf nodded in agreement. "Yes," he said. "We must get back before the Hohokam hear that most of our men are away from the cliff. Let us send a group of our fastest runners. They will wait until the rest of us arrive, and scout for the arrival of the Hohokam from this land.

The cliff's attackers must not discover that our men are away. If more Hohokam approach the Great Cliff, our runners must decide whether to fight. We would still have surprise on our side. If success is possible, we would have to attack."

Attack! Fight! Excitement and fear pumped through Blaze's body. This was what he had always dreamed of. Fighting for glory! Fighting to protect his people! But Blaze thought about the price of defeat, and suddenly, the allure of war faded. Real war was not a game. Guayball might be similar to a battle, but it was different because everyone walked away from a guayball game. And if they fought the Hohokam, they would be fighting against full grown men, men who would be trying to kill them.

"We should have at least one elder in the group," Dark Wolf said. "A decision might be needed which will determine the fate of our people."

"Who can keep pace with the young people?" Corn Grower asked.

"I can," Swift Deer said. "I was named for the fleet-footed animal and the spirit of the deer chose me as well. My animal spirit will aid me now."

My father? Impossible, Blaze thought. He could never keep up. He does nothing but tend the fields!

"Yes," Dark Wolf said to Swift Deer. "As a young man, you were the fastest in the village. You go along with Blaze, Long Horn, Running Stream, Sharp Stone, Tall Corn and Spear Thrower. The rest of us will follow as quickly as we can."

My father had been the fastest in the village? It is hard to believe, Blaze thought.

"Let us eat quickly," Swift Deer said with authority to the younger men. "We will travel day and night, sleeping only in short stretches."

The elders gave most of their weapons to the young men going on ahead. After a quick meal of bread, meat and nuts, Blaze's father led the small group forward as night was beginning to fall.

Blaze turned and saw most of the tribe elders standing with hands raised in farewell. These were the people who had taught him about Sinagua life. Sharp Stone's father Coyote Claw had taught him how to craft weapons and hunt. Swift Wing had taught him how to grow and collect food. Bighorn and Rattlebone had taught him about the gods below, and about the great cycle of life on this world. Setting Sun's father, Tall Grass, had loved him like a son. They had all danced the Dance of Rain each year, and given him gifts. He prayed that he would see them all again.

Swift Deer led the young men across the dry, rocky land. While they were not traveling as quickly as Blaze had gone alone, they were walking rapidly and without stops. In no time, darkness blanketed the sky. Swift Deer continued to lead the way through foreign land without hesitation. Blaze wondered how his father knew his way so well in Anasazi territory. Finally, after traveling most of the night, Swift Deer stopped.

"We can go further," Running Stream said.

"Yes," Swift Deer said, "but we will need the energy tomorrow. We will sleep until the first light of Father Sun, and then continue onward. We are nearly to the river."

Swift Deer spoke in a way that made no one question him. As a worker of the land, Swift Deer had always been knowledgeable, serious and sure of his ideas. Blaze was impressed that his father showed the same qualities leading his people on this all-important journey.

The seven travelers each ate lightly and lay down on the ground to sleep. Blaze knew that he should be tired after so much walking and running, but he could not go to sleep. There was too much to think about, too much to worry about. He was sure that he would lie awake the remainder of the night when suddenly a voice rang in his ears.

"Let's go!" Swift Deer commanded.

Blaze's eyes were drawn to the brightness low in the eastern sky. Morning! He had fallen asleep after all!

"Quickly, eat and drink. We must move!"

The men and boys quietly and quickly ate from their food bags and in no time were ready to continue their journey. By the time the sun was a fist above the horizon, they were at the river and moving south. Blaze and his tribesmen saw no Anasazi, but Blaze knew that his traveling party was being watched. By day's end, he was sure that they would be coming to Running River's home. At each bend in the river, Blaze expected to see their adobe dwelling.

Moving along a straight stretch of land surrounded by green, they heard a voice call out from a cluster of bushes.

"Blaze!"

Instantly Blaze's tribesmen each grabbed a weapon.

"It's all right," Blaze said, recognizing the voice. It was his young Anasazi friend.

Cautiously, the young boy stepped out from behind a leafy groundsel.

"Running River!" Blaze called out.

"My father told me to wait here to greet you. We were expecting you."

"Father," Blaze said, "this is Running River of the Anasazi tribe."

"I am Swift Deer. I am pleased to meet you. The Anasazi are good people."

"Please, come quickly to my home."

Running River ran along the river while Blaze and his fellow travelers followed. Shortly, they approached the adobe house that Blaze remembered so fondly. Black Bear and the other Anasazi men stood in front of the dwelling to greet them.

"I am Black Bear of the Anasazi," the large, bushy haired man said to the group.

"I am Swift Deer of the Sinaguas."

The two men nodded to each other.

"Six Hohokam came through today on their way to the Great Cliff. They had heard that most of the men of your tribe were hunting up here in our land. You must move quickly to get to your people."

"But the Hohokam will arrive there first!" Blaze cried. And it will be too late by then, he thought. They will know that just old men, women and children are defending the Great Cliff, and they will attack. They will also be prepared to defend against us as we get there. We will lose the element of surprise if there is a fight.

"You can get there sooner," Black Bear said. "The Hohokam are traveling the water route. The more direct route is there." The Anasazi elder pointed to the south, towards the flat desert.

"Can we make it without water?"

"If you bring enough and travel by the cool of night."

"Then that is what we will do."

"Fill your water bags here. We have extra water for you to bring, and extra food, too. There is little game on the route you will travel. If you move quickly, you should be at your home by sundown tomorrow."

"Thank you," Swift Deer said as the men and women of Running River's village handed over bags of food and water they had prepared. "We are eternally grateful. I hope that we have the opportunity to repay you in the future."

Black Bear nodded.

"Farewell," Swift Deer said.

"Goodbye, Running River," Blaze said.

As day grew into night, Swift Deer led the group at an even faster pace. Everyone was becoming weary, even Blaze. How was his father able to keep going? Yet Swift Deer did not stop. They traveled the entire night, eating as they walked, and alternately walking and running. Father Sun arose to greet them as they came upon familiar land.

"Father," Blaze asked, "how did you know how to travel through foreign lands in the dark?"

"The stars above," Swift Deer said. "When you can read the stars, then traveling in the night is as easy as traveling in the day, sometimes easier. The stars are a map. Know that map and never be lost."

Blaze had no idea that his father knew so much about traveling. He thought about the world of stars, and could not believe that there was any pattern, never mind a map that could direct people in their travels below. Blaze loved studying the maps that were painted on the lower levels of the Great Cliff. After each journey, the elders added to the painted maps showing the trails connecting the peoples of the earth. If they survived, he would ask his father to teach him to read the map of the stars.

By midday, they stopped. Swift Deer ordered the young men to shut their eyes for a short time. When Long Horn objected, Swift Deer told him that it was essential that they be at their sharpest when they reached the cliff. Besides, they did not want to arrive there before dark.

After a short daytime rest, Swift Deer roused the young men awake. "Let us move," he said.

Blaze looked with new eyes at his father. Swift Deer was no longer the cautious and dependable grower of food. He was a leader of men. In times of peace, his father had devoted himself entirely to tending the fields, and no one was more knowledgeable. In times of war, Swift Deer had shown himself to be an equally strong and wise leader. Blaze was comforted knowing that his father was in charge. His people were in good hands.

CHAPTER 29

▼

Blaze crept forward as quietly as he could. A thick layer of clouds dimmed any light from the stars and moon above. That was good. The Hohokam guards would never see him as he approached the cliff.

It made sense that he had been asked to scout the area. He was the only one who had seen the Hohokam camp. He was also the smallest, and could move most quietly. Still, it pleased him that Swift Deer had entrusted him with this most important assignment.

Blaze did not have to get very close to realize that the Hohokam were still camped at the foot of the cliff. They had not attacked! His people were safe! Slowly and carefully, Blaze turned around and quietly made his way back to the others. As he stepped into the cavelike opening under the rocky ledge, his tribesmen were all eagerly awaiting his news.

"We made it in time!" Blaze whispered. "They must not have heard that our men are all away. They are still waiting at the foot of the cliff trail."

"Lookouts?" Swift Deer asked.

"I think it's the same as before. Two at the foot of the trail and one guarding the rear of the camp."

Swift Deer nodded.

"We must attack!" Running Stream said.

"Yes," Long Horn and Tall Corn agreed.

Sharp Stone and Spear Thrower nodded as well.

"You are right, we cannot wait," Swift Deer said. "In a day, they will know that our men are not on the cliff. Blaze, how many were in the enemy party?"

"About twenty, I think," Blaze said.

"But they won't expect us," Running Stream said. "We will have the element of surprise on our side."

"True," Swift Deer said. "And what do you propose? Shall we kill them all in their sleep?"

There was silence. Blaze had not thought that far ahead. What should they do?

"If they were in our sandals, they would kill us," Running Stream argued.

Swift Deer took in the words but said nothing for a moment. All eyes were on the Sinagua leader. Finally, the giant elder spoke.

"If we kill them defenseless as they sleep, what do you think will happen when their tribesmen discover what we did?"

"They might not find out," Blaze said.

"If there are twenty or thirty Hohokam warriors here, with just seven of us, it will be difficult to make sure that none escape. If one man gets out, there will be five hundred Hohokam braves here by the next moon looking to kill every man, woman and child of the Great Cliff. Many of you have traveled to Hohokam land. They are a tribe of great numbers. Even if we killed all these men, others will come here and guess what happened. They would never let the disappearance of so many tribesmen go unavenged."

"Father, what else can we do?"

After thinking a moment, Swift Deer said, "We will take their weapons and make them leave."

"They will just come back," Running Stream said.

"We will make them promise to stay away."

"You cannot trust a Hohokam!" Running Stream said. "You saw what they did about our hunting agreement!"

"Most Hohokam are honorable people. I think that they would keep their word."

"And if they don't?" Running Stream asked.

"By that time, our cliff will be well fortified, and we will have all of our men to defend our home. If we are still at the Great Cliff."

"We might not be?" Blaze asked. He could not imagine life anywhere else.

"Blaze," Swift Deer said, "we have not always been here."

"I know. Where were we before?"

"We were not all together before the cliff. Our people were originally Anasazi, Hohokam, and Mogollan people, all in search of a new and better home. They came together at the well, and then moved to the cliff. They each brought their own way of life and their own language, and they came together to form the customs and language of the people of the Great Cliff."

"Is that why we understand the languages of all the surrounding tribes so well, and why they can understand us?"

"Yes," Swift Deer replied.

"I thought that we would always live at the Great Cliff," Blaze said.

"If we find that we cannot survive at the cliff, we will move on to new lands, richer in soil and rain. It is the way of the peoples of the earth. We do what is necessary to survive. Let us not worry about staying at or leaving the Great Cliff. If we do not deal with our Hohokam enemies effectively and wisely, there will be no one to stay or leave."

"Swift Deer," Spear Thrower asked. "How will we capture their weapons?"

"First, we must take out their guards. We must do it quickly and quietly. If we can do that, then the rest will be easy. After removing their guards, everyone except Running Stream will quietly approach their sleeping area, and each will put a spear to the neck of a sleeping enemy brave. We will try to do this to the six outermost men of their cluster."

"What will I do?" Running Stream asked.

"You will throw a torch in the middle of their sleeping group, and then run in circles around them, making the noise of twenty warriors. That way, all the Hohokam will be in the middle, between us. They will feel trapped. With the bright torch among them, we will see them better than they see us. And they will not see you, Running Stream, at all. They will believe that there are many of us prepared to attack. If any of the other warriors resist, Running Stream will use his bow to shoot the first to rise against us. If that does not stop them, we will kill the men at our hands, and then fire spears and arrows at the rest of the enemy braves."

"Why can't we try to take away their weapons as they sleep?" Sharp Stone asked.

"We might get some, but each Hohokam will have arrows or knives or spears attached to their breechcloth, even as they sleep. At some point, they would surely awaken. It must be done my way."

"Father, what if a guard cries out to warn them?" Blaze asked.

"Then we fight until the cause is lost. If you are alive then, retreat."

"We can beat them!" Running Stream said.

"They are warriors, my young, brave friend. We are not. That is why we must take out the guards quietly and then surprise the rest."

We would be warriors, too, if you and the elders had trained us, Blaze thought, but he found it hard to be angry with his father at that moment.

"Let me go after the lone guard facing the plains," Blaze said.

"Yes," Swift Deer said. "He will be closest to the rest of the warriors in their camp, and so you must be especially quiet. You must knock your man unconscious. If he moves at all, slit his throat."

Blaze swallowed hard and nodded.

"Long Horn, you and I will take out the cliff path guards. Blaze, we will wait for a signal from you. After you have silenced your guard, make the hoot of the night owl, and we will attack our guards."

"What about me?" Running Stream asked.

"If there is more than one plains guard, Blaze will need your help and he will caw like a crow and you will go to him. Otherwise, I will need you to be close to the center of camp. If they awaken early, I trust that you will attack as many of the enemy as possible. You will lead the attack and fight until you die. If you wound or kill enough, the rest of us might have a chance in a fight."

"You can count on me, Swift Deer."

"I know I can, Running Stream. I hope that I do not have to. The less blood we shed, the greater the chance our people have to survive. Remember that."

All six young men nodded earnestly.

"Are you ready?" Swift Deer asked.

"Yes," they all answered.

"Great Father below, aid us in this just battle that we fight. Father Sun, Father Corn, give us strength and wisdom. Blaze, Long Horn, are you ready?"

The two young men nodded.

"Blaze, you go. Long Horn, follow me."

Wielding a knife in one hand and a large rock in the other, Blaze turned around and cautiously stepped toward the enemy camp. Moving soundlessly over the hard terrain and staying low to the ground, he was sure that he would remain hidden in the shadows of the hills behind him.

Blaze could barely see a step ahead, but he knew every bump and crack in this ground from the countless times he had walked it as a child. Blaze was sure that he could make his way up the path completely blind. On such a dark night, he was almost blind. He stepped quietly toward the lookout ledge until he could make out the outline of a Hohokam guard.

Was it just one guard? Blaze was not sure. He was about thirty paces away from the guard and needed to get closer. He recognized the outline of a body and head, but could not tell which way the man was facing. Still crouched, Blaze crept forward.

Moving closer to the shadowed figure, Blaze felt he could almost strike the man with a spear. Taking another step forward, his left foot came down on a small stone. He raised his foot quickly but he heard the stone roll ever so slightly.

The guard quickly moved and then stood still. Blaze froze. He must be looking right at me, Blaze thought. Having approached from the direction of the low canyon wall, Blaze had stayed close enough to the ground so that there would be no backlight to expose even a shadow of himself. But the outline of the Hohokam guard now made it clear that he was staring straight at Blaze.

Blaze did not dare breathe. He ached to fill his lungs with air, but he knew that he couldn't. His people depended on him. And then the enemy guard moved. He stepped down from the low ledge and began walking.

He's coming right at me, Blaze thought. Does he see me?

And then the Hohokam guard stopped about one arm's length away. Blaze was sure that the man *had* to see him, but if he did, why did he not do anything? Blaze wanted to draw back his hand holding the rock, but they were so close that the man would be able to feel the air from any movement at all. Instead, Blaze remained frozen. He squeezed the knife in his left hand and the rock in his right. Another step by the man, and Blaze would have to attack.

But the dark figure did not move. Still low to the ground, Blaze's head was just below the waist of the man standing before him. He must be looking higher, above me, Blaze thought. The enemy guard seemed to stand there forever. The large rock in Blaze's hand grew heavier and heavier. It seemed to pull his whole body forward, but he had to fight that pull. And then the man's feet shuffled.

Which way was he moving? And then Blaze knew. The guard was coming right at him!

Instantly, Blaze sprung up and bashed his rock into the side of the man's head. The Hohokam uttered a quiet groan while Blaze lunged around the falling body to grab him before he hit the ground. He was a full grown adult and Blaze could barely hold him up. Blaze's knees buckled as he fell backwards trying to lower the limp body. The weight of his large enemy almost crushed him as he finally fell rear first onto the ground. Blaze lay on his back with his motionless enemy on top of him. Had any Hohokam heard them fall?

Blaze struggled to breathe. He could not pull himself out from beneath the smothering weight on his chest. Instead Blaze quietly rocked himself left to right until the body on top of him rolled off. Afraid to move, Blaze stared at his still victim and strained his ears to listen. Was his enemy still alive? Was he conscious? Had anyone heard?

The night was completely quiet. Blaze uttered the hoot of an owl as he crawled to the man he had just struck. Bringing his knife to the man's throat, Blaze strained to see his face. It was too dark to see very much, but if his enemy made the slightest movement, Blaze was prepared to kill him.

Just then, two hoots of an owl sounded from the ledge path. His father and Long Horn had taken out their two guards.

Blaze sighed in relief as he pulled his knife away from the throat of the man before him. The chest of the Hohokam moved up and down, indicating that he was still alive. Blaze did not want to kill a man, especially a defenseless one. As he stepped towards the enemy camp, he could make out the shapes of the sleeping enemy braves lying in the open ground. Two shadowy figures approached from the ledge. They had to be his father and Long Horn. Blaze knew that the others would be coming in from the right. He stopped about five paces short of the sleeping warrior closest to him. In moments, all his people were in place. The Hohokam camp was surrounded.

Why did they have only three guards? They must have little respect for the Sinaguas as fighters, Blaze thought. Even if Setting Sun had escaped, they believed that only two young boys were out there. Certainly not enough to pose a threat.

Blaze approached the nearest sleeping body and held the tip of his knife blade a finger's width from the man's throat. Swift Deer raised his hand and then Sharp Stone lit his torch. As it burst into flames, he tossed the burning torch into the middle of the sleeping bodies. Instantly, voices arose and men sprung to their feet. The sleeping warrior below Blaze shook to life. Blaze pushed the sharp tip of his knife into the soft flesh below the man's chin. With his other hand, Blaze pinned the man's neck to the ground.

"Do not move!" Blaze yelled above the roar.

Meanwhile, Running Stream was scampering wildly outside the circle of his tribesmen, yipping and hooting. He really did sound like a war party of a whole village of men.

"Put down your weapons now!" Swift Deer commanded.

One Hohokam man stood and raised a spear. From the shadows of the outer circle, Running Stream fired his arrow. The upright enemy was struck in the chest and fell face first onto the ground.

"Stop or die!" Swift Deer commanded.

No one moved.

"Our weapons are yours," a man in the middle of the Hohokam camp finally spoke as he held out his arms to his side. One by one, the other Hohokam braves stood with their arms held straight out to their left and right.

"Blaze, collect their weapons," Swift Deer ordered.

Blaze tried to move, but was frozen with fear. Fear of having to kill, and fear of being killed.

"Blaze?" a familiar voice spoke.

It was Setting Sun! Blaze's heart leapt with joy.

Words came to him at last. "Setting Sun!"

"Long Horn," Swift Deer said, "you get their weapons."

Long Horn ran through the tight Hohokam cluster, taking away their knives, spears and arrows, and tossing them to the outside. After his man was disarmed, Blaze pulled back his knife and let him retreat to his people. With the fiery light from the torch, Blaze could make out the faces of the Hohokam men. Searching for Setting Sun, Blaze spotted a smaller figure near the middle of the Hohokam pack. The boy turned towards Blaze, but it was not Setting Sun. It was Stonah!

And then Blaze saw Setting Sun, lying at the far end of the circle. His hands seemed to be tied behind his back as he was struggling to sit up.

"Setting Sun!" Long Horn cried. He ran to cut the boy's hands free and pulled him up.

About twenty Hohokam stood motionless as Setting Sun staggered towards Blaze.

"My friend!" Setting Sun said.

"It is good to see you," Blaze said.

"It is even better for me to see you," Setting Sun said and smiled. "I feared that you would not return. I would have bet against it."

"Who is the leader?" Swift Deer asked the group before him.

"I am," the voice of an older man calmly answered.

"I am Swift Deer of the Sinaguas. Step out and show yourself."

A tall, older man stepped forward. Completely bald, he stood proudly and nodded to Swift Deer. "I am Lionclah of the Hohokam."

"Lionclah, I beg your forgiveness for any lives we have taken."

"You did what was required for your people," the Hohokam leader responded. "Our lives are now all in your hands. Do what you feel is just."

"You came to the Great Cliff to kill our people and take our land."

"We did not come to kill your people."

"But you came to take our land. Did you think that we were going to just hand it over to you? You must have been prepared to kill us for it."

The shoulders of the noble chief sank as he hung his head in silence. After a few moments, he said, "I ask your forgiveness. The gods have spoken here. We were wrong to come and fight. That is why your great army has won here. Have them step forward so that we may honor them."

Swift Deer nodded.

In a moment, Running Stream stepped out of the surrounding darkness.

"Where are the rest?" a voice cried out. It was Bravegart!

"There are no more," Running Stream said.

"We handed our weapons to seven Sinaguas?" young Bravegart cried.

"Be quiet!" Lionclah commanded.

"But look! They have killed our brother!"

"Son, be quiet!" another man ordered.

Blaze looked to the man who had just spoken and saw that it was Greatgart. The powerful warrior glared at his son as Bravegart dropped his head in silence. Blaze let his eyes take in the entire scene before him. One Hohokam man lay on the ground, surrounded by twenty warriors standing with arms out to each side and hands wide open. Swift Deer and his young armed Sinaguas formed a circle around the enemy braves. Blaze's eyes met Stonah's, and his friend smiled to him. Blaze nodded and smiled in return.

"We want no more death," Swift Deer said. "You may all leave now. Take food and water, but leave your weapons with us. Promise to leave and never return. Tell your people that the Sinaguas wish you no harm. We only wish to be left in peace."

"You are more than just," the Hohokam leader said. "I agree to go from your cliff and I give you my word that we will not come back."

"You have a band of hunters coming this way from Anasazi land," Swift Deer said.

"I will send a messenger to meet them and tell them of your fair treatment of us," the Hohokam leader said. "They will leave you in peace."

"Is your man alive?" Swift Deer asked, nodding his head to the fallen brave.

Lionclah approached the body lying face down on the ground, and squatted before him. After a brief examination, Lionclah quietly stated, "He is dead. We will take him with us and bury him with his own people."

"Spear Thrower, Tall Corn, Long Horn," Swift Deer ordered, "go get their guards."

The three young men went off and in moments returned, dragging the fallen Hohokam guards.

"Are they dead?" Bravegart asked.

"They are all breathing," Tall Corn said.

Bravegart finally turned to Blaze and stared angrily at him. In spite of his fear, Blaze returned Bravegart's murderous glare with a stonelike expressionless. Greatgart grabbed Bravegart's arm and quietly said, "Come."

"We can care for your injured men until they are healthy," Swift Deer said. "We have a fine medicine woman."

"We will take them with us," Lionclah answered.

Three Hohokam men grabbed their unconscious tribesmen, and carried them off. One by one, the rest of the Hohokam boys and men passed by Blaze. Some he remembered seeing from his journey. Most he did not. Finally, Stonah stood before him.

"Take care, my friend," Blaze murmured. "You belong in your land of great cities and ball arenas, not on a cliff which could house so few of you."

"We are leaving Snaketown," Stonah said. "There are too many of us and there is not enough food. That is why we were seeking a new home. Our people are leaving the great Hohokam world in search of greener land."

"Tell Shinestah that I shall remember her fondly."

Stonah nodded and whispered, "Goodbye, Blaze of the Great Cliff."

"Goodbye, Stonah."

Shortly, the Hohokam were all gone.

"Spear Thrower," Swift Deer said, "go to the cliff and tell our people that we have returned."

Sprinting up the path, he called out loudly for all to hear, "Spear Thrower approaching the first ledge!"

Blaze was home and his people were safe. He lay on the ground and let his eyes fall shut. He wondered if he would ever see Stonah or Shinestah again. Or Bravegart. He prayed that his path would never cross that of his angry young enemy.

Hearing footsteps approach, Blaze looked up into the face of his longtime friend. Setting Sun was dirty and thin, but his eyes sparkled with joy. Blaze did not have the energy to say a word. He wanted to know what had happened to his friend after they had separated, but that story could wait.

Cries of joy sounded from the cliff. Blaze thought of how happy his mother would be when she saw him. It warmed his heart. He just wanted to be with his mother and his sisters and his grandfather. At that moment, Swift Deer came from behind and put his arm around Blaze. He squeezed Blaze firmly, then let go, and walked on towards the cliff. Blaze wanted to be home with his father as well. He followed Swift Deer up the ledge path to his people and his home.

CHAPTER 30

▼

"Father Corn," Great Bear's voice echoed through the Great Room, "we thank you for this home and its great walls which have protected us and have kept us warm. We thank you for the surrounding soil which for generations has blessed us with plentiful crops."

Silence followed. Even the young children and babies were quiet. True, they were well fed. Blaze could never remember eating so much himself. They had planned to remain longer at the cliff, and so there was more food still remaining than they could carry with them. Thus, all had been ordered to eat heartily. After a winter of carefully limited portions of food, it was an order that had been easy to follow. Blaze's stomach almost hurt from eating so much bread, meat, corn and beans. But the silence came from more than just full bellies. Even the young ones could sense the momentousness of the event.

This would be the last time that all the Sinagua people would gather in the Great Room. Blaze wondered if they would ever again find a home quite like this. Probably not. Travelers had often marveled at their spectacular cliff dwelling. Blaze looked with sadness at his image on the wall. He, Spear Thrower and Setting Sun still adorned the wall in brightly colored, bigger-than life fashion. How long would that spectacular painting by Deer Eyes decorate the Great Room? Would he ever see it again?

Golden Eagle stood and sang, "Father Sun, Father Corn, we ask you to guide us safely in our journey to a new home. Lead us to a place where we will continue to be nourished and safe, a place where we may remain one people."

Golden Eagle was the oldest member of the tribe, yet he could still sing beautifully. His deep, crackly voice filled the Great Room. His words of prayer would surely make their way to the gods below.

Blaze looked across the room and saw his mother and two sisters seated on the ground with the other women and children. Blaze had so often dreamt of sitting with the village men for the ceremonies in the Great Room, and he was with them at last. He was a man of his tribe. He had so often imagined climbing up the cliff ladders wearing his mask and feathers for the Dance of Rain, but that would never happen. They would be far from this cliff for the next Dance of Rain.

Blaze put that thought out of his mind, and instead savored the present moment. He was sitting in the Great Room as a man among his tribesmen. His father was at his side. His grandfather should be sitting on his other side. At least his grandfather would never suffer the pain of leaving this cliff which had been his home for all the harvests of his long life.

Lion Heart had died in his sleep early in the winter. He must have known that he was going to die, because he had talked to Blaze for much of that last day. His grandfather had spoken about his many ancestors who had gone on to the Great Underground. He had talked about the way their courage and wisdom had contributed so much to the welfare of the tribe. Blaze was not surprised when he heard that Lion Heart had died in the night. He missed his grandfather, but his passing to the Great Underground seemed as natural as going to sleep and waking up.

At last, Great Bear gave the word to move from their home in the Great Cliff. They would journey north, where travelers had said that the sun was not so hot and water was in greater abundance.

The women and children led the march out of the Great Room, and climbed down the ladders of the cliff one final time. The women from Great Bear's family left first, followed by Black Rabbit and her four children. Her oldest, Sharp Stone, would be a man soon. Sharp Stone had shown great skill and courage for the Upper Cliff pod over the winter, and would surely be a village leader before too many harvests elapsed. He held his guayball close to his chest, as did many of the boys. The grand elders had decided to allow guayball once again. They even encouraged it in hopes of training the young people to better defend themselves should war be necessary. Lion Heart had helped to convince the other elders that guayball would be good for the people of Sinagua.

Blaze's mother climbed out the door next. Attached to her side was a red woven bag that held the bones of Blaze's dead brothers. Lightfoot was followed by Bay Leaf, who carried Chittanberry on her back. The clan of women from Golden Eagle's third floor family went out after Blaze's family. Golden Eagle's wife, White Tail, was almost as old as Desert Cloud, but after a lifetime of working the fields, she still moved like a young person. The rest of the women and children headed to the doorway. Desert Cloud was the last of the women to leave. She could barely walk, yet down she went. Blaze wondered if she had the strength to travel to a new land. Tall Corn followed close behind her. Over the winter, she had designated Tall Corn to be her apprentice. He would learn the ways of medicine from her. Tall Corn would not provide the game from hunting that Blaze always had, but he did have a good mind for the complex mix of medicinal ingredients, and a good memory for the healing chants. His father Great Bear was very proud of him. Blaze had a feeling that Desert Cloud would will herself to live long enough to teach Tall Corn all she knew.

The young men of the tribe went out next. Most had grown to love guayball. They had played much throughout their last winter in the Great Cliff, and had become a skilled and ferocious group of competitors. Blaze was sad that he would never have the chance to bring these men to the Hohokam arenas to do battle. He was sure that his people would triumph. They had learned to play as one, with skill, heart and wisdom. Large Rock, Spear Thrower, Strong Horn, Running Stream and Fleet Foot moved out together. Along with the older boys, Setting Sun, Sharp Stone and Tall Corn, they had formed the two rival pods of the Great Cliff.

Descending the ladders he had moved up and down so many times, it did not seem possible that this would be Blaze's last time down. A rush of sadness overwhelmed him, but the thought of unknown lands and new adventures excited him as well. At the bottom ledge, he looked up at the men still moving down the ladders. Blaze did not want to leave. This had been a great home, and he wanted to stay, but he knew that they must go.

Swift Deer took his last step off the ladder and walked towards Blaze. He stopped in front of his son and stood eye to eye with him. Blaze had grown to be as tall as his father, and they stood as equals. Blaze could see the sadness in his father's soft gray eyes, and knew that leaving was especially hard for him. His father had put his whole life into making this cliff and the surrounding fields a safe and comfortable home for his people. He loved the land he had tended with such care. Swift Deer reached out and grasped Blaze by the shoulders. He held his son firmly but said nothing. Yet through his father's strong hands, Blaze could feel the love Swift Deer felt for him.

At last, his father let go and marched down the ledge path with his son by his side. At the base of the path, the people of the village were picking up the belongings they would take to their new home. They all were required to bring food. Blaze smiled when he saw Setting Sun's bulging waist sack. Beads! What a waste of space! But Setting Sun loved the beads he had worked so hard to win. Swift Deer loaded himself with tools that would help him tend the fields in their new home, and with seeds to grow their new crops. Tall Corn was weighted down with bags of ingredients for the tribe's medicines. Golden Eagle, his son Rattle Bone, and Rattle Bone's son Hard Shell each had layer upon layer of their beautifully woven cloth tied to their backs. Women and men hauled pots and tools. Along with food, Blaze carried a large bag of arrowheads around his waist, along with a quiver full of arrows. He also brought long spears for hunting and short spears for fighting. And of course he had his golden sun necklace and his mountain lion guayball.

There was a chill in the air as his tribe headed northward. They had decided to leave before winter was done, hoping to make a new home for themselves before planting season. No one was talking. Each man, woman and child seemed as lost in their memories as Blaze. Finally, Blaze turned to give his home one last look. The empty dwellings in the Great Cliff appeared sad and majestic at the same time. Blaze wondered if he would ever see this awesome structure again.

And then he turned away from the cliff one final time, determined not to be sad and not to look back. Instead, Blaze began to dream of the life before him. Would his people build another home in a cliff? Or would they live in adobe huts, as the Anasazi did? Would there be enough food on their journey and in their new home? Would the gods below still look after them in their new world? Would Blaze ever see his friend Stonah again? Would he ever see Bravegart, and would he have to fight him some day? Blaze wondered if he would grow to be a leader of his people. If so, he prayed that he would lead his people wisely in war or peace. He wondered if he would some day see Shinestah. He had a feeling that he would.

Blaze stepped down from the cliff path to the flat land below, and began his journey to a new life.

Author's Note

While the tribes in this story did exist, the novel is a work of fiction. Nevertheless, the people and their way of life are portrayed as accurately as possible. The ancient Native American people of the desert lived in the land we now know as Arizona. They did not refer to themselves as Sinagua, Hohokam or Anasazi. Those names were given to the tribes by the European explorers who later came to those lands. Because none of these ancient people had a written language, we do not know what they called themselves. In this story, for lack of anything closer to the truth, the desert tribes refer to themselves by the names we call them today.

The Great Cliff is an actual cliff dwelling known as Montezuma Castle. It was so named because European settlers mistakenly thought it had been built by Aztec people for their emperor, Montezuma. It is one of the most spectacular and best preserved cliff dwellings in the American southwest. The Sinagua people lived in Montezuma Castle from approximately 1100 AD to 1400 AD. No one knows why the great cliff dwellings were abandoned or what occurred in the final days. This novel tells what might have happened.

Other children's novels by Mark Fidler:

Signed Ball
Baseball Sleuth
Zamboni Brez

plus the award winning novels *Pond Puckster* and *The Call of Sagar-matha*

For more information about these books, see www.markfidler.com

Printed in the United States
205030BV00002B/151-573/A